A Coronation
of Love

Also by Barbara Cartland
in Large Print:

The Call of the Highlands
Lights, Laughter and a Lady
The Love Puzzle
A Song of Love
Bride to the King
A Duke in Danger
Ola and the Sea Wolf
A Caretaker of Love
Secret Harbor
From Hate to Love
The Prude and the Prodigal
A Night of Gaiety
A Kiss in Rome

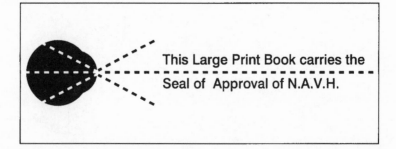

This Large Print Book carries the
Seal of Approval of N.A.V.H.

Barbara Cartland

A Coronation of Love

Thorndike Press • Waterville, Maine

Published in 2002 by arrangement with
International Book Marketing, Ltd.

Thorndike Press Large Print Paperback Series.

The tree indicium is a trademark of Thorndike Press.

The text of this Large Print edition is unabridged.
Other aspects of the book may vary from the original edition.

Set in 16 pt. Plantin by Myrna S. Raven.

Printed in the United States on permanent paper.

Library of Congress Cataloging-in-Publication Data

Cartland, Barbara, 1902–
    A coronation of love / Barbara Cartland.
      p. cm.
    ISBN 0-7862-4899-8 (lg. print : sc : alk. paper)
    1. Queens — Fiction. 2. Romanies — Fiction.
  3. Large type books. I. Title.
PR6005.A765 C67 2002
  823′.912—dc21
                                     2002035870

A Coronation
of Love

Author's Note

There are millions of Gypsies wandering about the world despite every effort by many countries in Europe to be rid of them.

But they still exist and they still have an important part to play in the history of civilisation.

The Gypsies came originally from India and a great number of words in their language, which is called "Romany," are of Indian origin.

The majority of the Gypsy legends describe them as smiths of various kinds, as well as workers in iron, gold, bronze, and precious stones.

I have seen the *Kalderash* in India, sitting at the sides of the roads with their black tents, the women wearing an enormous number of beautiful bracelets set with jewels as their men hammer away at various metals.

One Gypsiologist said:

"It seems certain that it was the Gypsies who made bronze known in Europe."

He cites the fact that some excavations along the Baltic have brought to light weapons and pieces of jewellery ornamented with the swastika which is known to be of Indian origin.

According to tradition of the *Kalderash* Gypsies, some groups of Gypsies, who were smiths responsible for the maintenance of working stock, followed the Tartar armies on their moves from place to place.

One of the legends of this group even specifies that by way of gain, they had the right to collect everything that remained in the villages after a week of pillage.

One of the great authorities, MacMunn, says:

The Bohemians of Europe, without any doubt, followed the armies of the Huns, Tartars and Seljuks, and our own Gypsies who work in metals and grind our knives certainly sharpened swords and blades for the armies who traversed Europe in every sense.

Romany Gypsies, wherever they go, still have the dark hair, the dark eyes, and the slightly dark skin which makes one sure that they came from the East.

They have been persecuted in almost every European country.

They arrived in England at the time of Henry VIII, and at one time they were moved every twenty-four hours by the Police.

This went on until I had the Law changed in 1964 so that every Gypsy child could go to School.

It was a bitter battle that lasted for three years, until in 1964 the Home Secretary, Sir Keith Joseph, wrote to me and said that I had won my battle.

He had issued an edict that every Local Authority must provide camps for their own Gypsies.

Now thousands and thousands of Gypsy children go to School, and in my County, which is Hertfordshire, there are fourteen camps, and I have my own camp which I set up for just one family of Romanies the year that the law was altered.

chapter one

1887

Queen Aldrina of Saria wanted to scream.

She had hoped that the almost hour-long dissertation from the Prime Minister had come to an end.

But just as she was hoping she would be able to go out into the sunshine, he started again.

He was talking of matters concerning which she had no knowledge.

She had to clench her fingers to prevent herself from stopping him from saying any more.

She thought that no one could be so dull for so long, nor say so much without imparting any information which was of the least interest.

At last the Prime Minister was saying:

"That is my opinion, Your Majesty."

The Queen was just about to say that that ended the Privy Council, when the Secretary of State for Foreign Affairs rose.

"I think, Your Majesty," he said, "we should make it quite clear in some way or another, without being aggressive, that we strongly disapprove of the behaviour of Prince Terome of Xanthe."

"Why?" the Queen asked.

"Because, Your Majesty, the Prince is behaving in the most outrageous fashion, and it would be a great mistake for our country to ignore it, or to appear indifferent to the things that are happening in Xanthe."

"What things?" the Queen asked.

It was the first time anything had been said that morning which sounded in the least interesting.

The Secretary of State for Foreign Affairs coughed and looked uncomfortable.

"There are things, Your Majesty," he said, "which are impossible to explain to you."

"Because I am half-witted?" the Queen asked. "Or merely because I am a woman?"

The Privy Counsellors sat up at the way she spoke and looked at her reproachfully.

She was well aware that the majority of them, who were all over fifty, regretted that a woman should be ruling the country.

But there was nothing they could do about it.

The Queen had been sent at the age of eighteen by Queen Victoria to Saria.

It was considered important by the British Government that any country with a coastline on the Aegean Sea should have British support.

Aldrina had come to be the bride of the King.

She had been very frightened at leaving England and everything that was familiar.

At the same time, it was exciting to think that she would reign in a country, however small.

It was also, she knew, near Greece.

The Greek legends and the History of Ancient Greece had been one of her favourite interests ever since she was small.

But when she reached Saria, she found everything was very different from what she had expected.

First of all, there was no ardent Bridegroom to meet her as the Battleship docked in the small Port that served the whole country.

She was informed by the Prime Minister and other Ministers of State that His Majesty was indisposed.

They hoped, however, that it was only for a short time.

Their hopes were not to be realised.

Because the Doctors considered the King to be in a precarious state of health,

13

Aldrina was married to him at his bedside.

Then she was told that she must act as Queen of Saria until he was well enough to take his place at her side.

She was extremely disappointed at not being able to wear her elaborate and very expensive wedding-gown.

It had been provided for her by Queen Victoria because she was Her Majesty's God-daughter.

The Queen was well aware that it would be impossible for Aldrina's mother, who was very poor, to provide a suitable trousseau for a reigning Queen.

For the first time in her life she had lovely gowns, exquisite underlinen trimmed with lace, and hats she had never dreamed of possessing.

Aldrina had, however, given less thought to the fact that marriage must involve also a Bridegroom.

She would have a man to guide, protect, and make love to her.

She was not certain what this entailed.

She was very innocent and had no knowledge of men.

She and her mother had lived very quietly in a Grace and Favour apartment in Hampton Court Palace.

The only men she met were aged Ambassadors and retired Generals and Admirals.

But everything became exciting from the moment Queen Victoria told her she was to be married to a King.

There were the shops in Bond Street to visit.

She had in the past only been able to stare at their windows.

Statesmen came to the small house at Hampton Court.

They explained to her how she must uphold the importance of Britain in her new country.

Her mother's few friends sent letters of congratulation and wedding-presents.

It was only when Aldrina was sailing through the Mediterranean that she began to wonder seriously what her Bridegroom would look like.

She had been told, of course, that he was not a young man.

He had outlived two wives, neither of whom had provided him with an heir to the throne.

She thought that because he was of Greek origin, he would be tall and handsome, with dark hair and dark eyes.

Doubtless he would resemble the Greek gods who had figured in her dreams ever since she had first read about them.

Reality had been very different.

When she was taken to meet the man she was to marry, she found that he was bald-headed, with just a few white hairs.

His face was deeply lined and he spoke in a gruff, hesitating voice.

He did not apologise for his disability.

He merely ordered his Ministers who had accompanied Aldrina to the bedside to get on with the wedding and be quick about it.

"If you do not hurry," he said harshly, "you will have that young swine Prince Inigo taking my place and, God knows, you do not want him!"

There was a murmur of assent from the Ministers.

Aldrina was informed that the marriage would take place in two days' time.

The appearance of her Bridegroom was such a shock that she was thankful there was no question of his making love to her.

He merely growled out his responses during the Marriage Ceremony.

He then closed his eyes and said he wanted to go to sleep.

It was three weeks before he died.

Aldrina paid him, every day, a dutiful visit, during which he said very little to her.

She was intelligent enough to realise that the King had wanted another wife only to give him an heir.

As, however, he was now incapable of leaving his bed, she was no longer of any consequence to him.

What she did find frightening was that when he died she was told she had to reign over Saria in his place.

She had not the slightest idea how to go about it.

It was, however, something that need not have worried her.

From the moment she woke in the morning to the time she went to bed, there were always people to tell her what to do, and more people to make sure she did it.

What she had not expected was the way Prince Inigo presented himself.

He demanded to see her the day after the King's Funeral.

It had been a very impressive ceremony and the streets were lined with mourners.

The Funeral procession was nearly a mile long, and the flags were at half-mast.

The Band played a "Death March" all the way to the Cathedral.

After the long-drawn-out ceremony the King was buried in a Royal vault.

The Queen was driven back to the Palace.

Dressed in her widow's weeds with a dark veil over her face, she could look out at the people without being noticed.

They were not aware that she was curious.

On her return to the Palace she was forced to listen to long speeches of condolence.

It was over two hours before she could go to her own apartments.

Even then there were two Ladies-in-Waiting with her.

Both of them sniffled into their handkerchieves because they thought it was expected of them.

It irritated Aldrina to find that the only time she could be alone was when she retired for the night.

It was a surprise and almost a relief when she was told that the Prince Inigo wished to see her.

She had learned that he had attended the Funeral.

But amongst a variety of men in uniform she was unable to pick out which one he was.

Now, as she saw him come into her Private Sitting-Room in his ordinary clothes, she was disappointed.

She had been hoping after the King's remarks about him that he would be somewhat nearer to her own age.

A quick glance told her that the Prince must be almost forty.

Although he was tall and dark, he was by no means handsome, nor had he any resemblance to the Greek gods of her dreams.

His face was debauched and there were heavy lines under his eyes.

There was a sharpness in the way he spoke which she disliked.

She was also certain that the expression in his eyes was hostile.

However, he bowed to her politely.

When she invited him to be seated, he sat in a chair near to hers.

"I suppose, Ma'am," he said, speaking in a hard, quick manner, as if he wished to get on with it, "you have heard about me?"

"Very little," Aldrina replied, "but then, I have been in Saria only a very short time."

"It is, of course," the Prince said, "a grave mistake on my Cousin's part to have married you in that absurd way on his death-bed."

Aldrina thought his manner was somewhat rude, and she replied a little hesitatingly:

"I . . . I am sure His Majesty . . . did not . . . realise how . . . ill he was when . . . he sent his Ambassador . . . to Queen Victoria to ask . . . for his Bride."

The Prince snorted — there was no other word for it.

"Saria does not need the help of the British," he said firmly. "We are perfectly secure, and it is all nonsense to believe that the Russians, or anyone else, may attack us."

"I understood," Aldrina replied, "that they have already invaded countries to the North of us."

"We are in the South!" the Prince snapped. "I do not believe half the things I hear."

There seemed to be no answer to that.

Aldrina sat silent until the Prince said:

"You must be aware what is the right thing for you to do now, considering you have come so far to wave the Union Jack."

"I . . . I do not . . . understand," Aldrina answered.

"I should have thought that the Prime Minister, or one of those stupid old men in the Privy Council, would have informed you that it is your duty to marry me!"

Aldrina stiffened and stared at him in astonishment.

She had thought when he entered the room that he was not a very pleasant man.

Now she was quite certain he was extremely unpleasant, and abominably rude.

For a moment she felt frightened.

Then she remembered that, after all, she was the Queen.

Slowly she rose to her feet.

"I think, Your Royal Highness," she said, "you have forgotten that I am in mourning for my husband. No question of my remarrying can arise for at least a year."

With that she walked from the room.

The door opened before she reached it.

An *Aide-de-Camp* who had been waiting outside had undoubtedly, she thought, been listening.

She was certain that their conversation would be relayed immediately to the Prime Minister.

No more than an hour after the Prince had left, the Prime Minister begged an audience with her.

By this time she had recovered her composure from the uncomfortable encounter with the Prince.

She therefore said before he could speak: "I cannot understand, Prime Minister, why you did not tell me that Prince Inigo wishes to reign in the King's place."

It was not difficult to deduce that that was why he was demanding that she should marry him.

It had been confirmed when she had enquired of one of her Ladies-in-Waiting, an elderly Baroness, as to what was Prince Inigo's position in the country.

"He was Heir Presumptive to His Late Majesty, Ma'am," the Baroness explained, "if he did not produce a son or have a wife."

Aldrina already knew why she had been married with such haste.

Her late husband, who had not even kissed her, had disliked the Prince as much as she did.

There was no doubt either about the Prime Minister's feelings.

He put it very tactfully.

"His Royal Highness, Ma'am, has never been popular with the people and, although I should not speak of it to you, he has been involved in many scandals which upset His Late Majesty. It made him say to me over and over again: 'Prince Inigo must not be allowed to sit on the throne.' "

Aldrina thought that settled the problem of Prince Inigo.

She had, however, reckoned without him.

He called the following day with a bouquet of flowers for her.

He also made a fulsome apology for having upset her.

"I assure you," he said in an ingratiating tone, "that I had no wish to do so. In fact, I really wanted to tell you that I am overwhelmed by your beauty and charm."

He smiled and then continued:

"My only desire is to help you as much as I can in ruling over my country, to which I am devoted."

This was a very different approach, but Aldrina was not deceived.

When she looked into his eyes, she realised they were hard.

There was no doubt in her mind that in the very last days of the King's life, Prince Inigo had been frustrated in his ambition to succeed him.

It was almost impossible to stop the Prince from wooing her.

The Prime Minister and the Privy Council as well as the other Statesmen might dislike him.

Yet he was still a member of the Royal Family.

There was nothing, therefore, that anybody could do to stop him from calling at the Palace.

Aldrina tried every possible way to avoid seeing him.

But nothing would stop him from insisting on an audience.

He could invite himself to luncheon or dinner.

He could insist on being present on every State occasion.

The Prime Minister had drawn up for Aldrina a programme which would enable her to get to know the people of the City.

Then there was the country itself.

There were Schools and Hospitals to visit, speeches to be made in public buildings.

There was a constant stream of deputations asking to be received.

On every occasion, it seemed, Prince Inigo turned up.

He would be magnificently attired in the uniform of a Field Marshal, to which he was not in fact entitled.

Covered in decorations and wearing a plumed hat, he could not be ignored.

He waved to the crowd, although they seemed indifferent.

He managed to stand as near to Aldrina as possible.

Finally she told the Prime Minister that she found the Prince's presence intolerable.

Something must be done about it, she insisted.

The Prime Minister, who was an elderly man, made a helpless gesture with his hands.

"I do not have due authority, Ma'am."

"Why not?" Aldrina enquired.

"Because, Ma'am, His Royal Highness is not doing anything actually wrong. He says he is helping you, though we all know what the ulterior motive is behind such attention."

The Prime Minister glanced at the Queen to see if she understood what he insinuated.

"I suppose .... Prime Minister," she said, "you realise that Prince Inigo . . . is determined . . . to marry me?"

The Prime Minister's expression was one of relief that he did not have to explain this to her.

"That is very obvious, Ma'am," he replied, "and I only hope you do not think it is something which our people desire, or our country needs."

"I have told His Royal Highness on frequent occasions that it is wrong and tact-

25

less of him to raise such a matter when I am still in mourning for the King. But who can . . . say what will . . . happen before . . . the year is . . . ended."

The Prime Minister looked worried.

It flashed through Aldrina's mind that the consequences were unthinkable.

The Prince might find some method of *forcing* her to marry him, however hard she tried to prevent it.

After a long pause the Prime Minister said:

"I will consider this matter carefully, Your Majesty, and perhaps I and my colleagues can come up with a solution to the problem."

Aldrina realised without his saying any more that he was not very confident there would be one.

She had read a great deal of history.

She could remember occasions when ambitious men had forced themselves upon women who were not strong enough to resist them.

They had been forced to capitulate, in some cases into what was nothing more than a condition of slavery.

"What . . . can I do? What can . . . I do?" she asked.

She was aware that the Prince's visits

were becoming more and more frequent.

She could feel the threat behind the compliment-strewn manner in which he addressed her.

She was thinking of Prince Inigo now when the Secretary of State for Foreign Affairs was speaking of Prince Terome.

"What is wrong with the Prince?" she asked bluntly.

The Foreign Secretary hesitated for a moment before he said:

"His Royal Highness does not really concern us, as his country is on the far side of the River Leeka. But there are, I understand, things taking place in Xanthe which might give rise to a revolution."

He paused and then said:

"This would undoubtedly be brought to the attention of the Russians. It could give them an excuse to invade the country to maintain order."

Aldrina had heard this argument before.

It was the fear of every small Balkan country that the Russians would invade them, ostensibly to ensure that they governed themselves competently.

"What does the Prince do?" she persisted.

The Foreign Secretary looked helplessly at his colleagues.

"As I have said, Ma'am," he replied, "the country is badly ruled, for the King does not keep a firm hand on what is occurring."

"Why? Is he ill?" the Queen enquired.

Again the Foreign Secretary looked at the other members of the Privy Council.

Then he said:

"I am afraid, Ma'am, the King over-indulges himself, and therefore the Prince, as heir to the throne, has a free hand in all he wishes to do."

The Queen gathered from this that the King drank.

Although she thought it was regrettable, she did not feel it affected Saria in any way.

"As you say," she remarked aloud, "Xanthe is on the other side of the River Leeka, and has no boundary with us."

She paused and then said:

"In fact, Ravalla lies between us and Xanthe and, as I have not heard you speak of that country, I presume it is well governed?"

"It is," the Prime Minister conceded. "At the same time, Ma'am, King Leander of Ravalla is continually away, travelling in other parts of the world. That is why our country is of such importance at the moment."

Aldrina could understand this.

It was more or less what the English Prime Minister had explained to her.

Queen Victoria had said sharply:

"It would be a great mistake to allow the Russians to expand any farther into the Balkans, and I have known for a long time that the only thing that prevented them from doing so is the attitude of Great Britain."

The Marquess of Salisbury, the Secretary of State for Foreign Affairs, had told Aldrina how ten years earlier the Russians had threatened to reach Constantinople.

They were within six miles of the City when four British Battleships had steamed into the Aegean Sea.

Their presence there had forced the Russians to withdraw.

It struck Aldrina now that they were expecting her to be as influential as four Battleships.

The idea made her want to laugh.

Aloud she said:

"I understand what you are saying, but I would like to know more. Please inform me in detail what excesses are taking place in Xanthe, and what danger the Crown Prince therefore is to us."

With that she rose to make it quite clear that the audience was at an end.

She was sure that as soon as she had left the room there would be long faces at what she had demanded.

They would certainly talk about it for hours, if not days.

She gave a little chuckle to herself, then ran up to her Sitting-Room.

It annoyed her to think that now it was time for luncheon.

It would be the usual long-drawn-out meal with the members of the Household and her Ladies-in-Waiting, none of whom would have anything new to say.

They followed her about, she thought, like a lot of dogs.

In fact, she often wished that was what they were.

She thought how lovely it would be if she could run out unattended into the garden, or, better still, to walk on a beach.

She loved the sea.

The greatest joy of her childhood had been when her mother had saved enough money so that they could rent a cheap house on the coast.

"That is what I would like to do now," Aldrina said to herself.

Then, as she went into her bed-room to tidy herself before luncheon, she had an idea.

It was an idea which, once in her mind, persisted all through luncheon.

As she had anticipated, it was a dreary meal.

She had not liked to make a lot of changes on her arrival at the Palace.

One of the things the King had apparently enjoyed was to have at least five or six *Aides-de-Camp* or other members of the Household with him at every meal.

Aldrina and her Ladies-in-Waiting had simply been a further addition to the numbers traditionally present.

She had been too nervous at first to suggest that they should do anything different.

But she would have preferred to eat quietly with only two or three people.

Then she could talk without being afraid of saying something indiscreet.

When Aldrina came out from luncheon it was three o'clock.

She was about to go into the garden when she was told that a Deputation was waiting for her in the Throne Room.

"I must have some fresh air!" she protested.

"Perhaps, Your Majesty, they will not stay for long," an *Aide-de-Camp* suggested.

"It is a lovely day, and I have not been outside for one moment!" Aldrina argued.

31

"I am going into the garden now, and the Deputation will have to wait!"

Even as she said so, she was aware it was rude.

It would certainly be disapproved of by the Prime Minister.

The *Aide-de-Camp,* who was a middle-aged man, looked on helplessly as Aldrina quickly walked away from him.

She hurriedly made her way to the hall, from where she could go out into the garden.

She had almost reached it when the Comptroller of the Household came hurrying after her.

"Your Majesty, Your Majesty," he cried, "there is a Deputation waiting in the Throne Room!"

"I am aware of that," Aldrina answered, "but I must have some air!"

"You are not feeling well?" he asked.

Aldrina clutched at the idea.

"No," she replied. "I am not at all well, and I would like to see a Doctor later to-day."

As the Comptroller of the Household stared at her in consternation, she was able to escape into the garden before he could say any more.

She was alone, for her Ladies-in-Waiting

were far behind her and were not aware of what was happening.

She ran across the green lawn and disappeared through some bushes that were heavy with blossom.

Just beyond some trees, she reached a part of the garden where she had never been before.

There were, she saw, shrubs which reminded her of those familiar to her in England.

Except for the song of the birds, it was very quiet.

There were butterflies hovering over the flowers and on the shrubs.

The sun was shining through the boughs of the trees which met overhead.

At last she felt free.

She told herself she could no longer endure feeling shackled in the Palace as she had been every day since the King had died.

'It is so dull!' she thought.

She walked on, feeling that with the buzz of the bees and the butterflies flitting ahead it was like being in Fairyland.

'I suppose I am being silly to let them imprison me as they do. I must get away, if only for a short while. Otherwise I shall scream as I wanted to scream this morning at the Privy Council!'

It was half-an-hour before she returned to the house to find a large group of Ministers and Ladies-in-Waiting, as well as attendants, waiting for her in the hall.

She guessed they had been debating as to how they should reprove her and prevent her from running wild another time.

Holding her head high, she said to the assembled throng:

"I now wish to see the Deputation, and I do not wish that more than two people should accompany me!"

The Ladies-in-Waiting and the Ministers all looked at each other in astonishment.

She walked ahead.

Finally one of the Ministers followed her, side by side with her Senior Lady-in-Waiting, who was well over sixty.

They had almost reached the door of the Throne Room when an *Aide-de-Camp* came hurrying down the passage.

He managed to reach the Queen before the footman opened the door for her.

"I beg your pardon, Your Majesty," he said, "but Prince Inigo has just arrived and wishes to accompany you while you receive the Deputation."

"Thank His Royal Highness for coming," the Queen replied, "and tell him that I have decided to receive the Deputation with only two people to accompany me."

There was a look of surprise on the *Aide-de-Camp*'s face.

There was also a look of dismay, as if he had no wish to carry such a message to the Prince.

Then the doors of the Throne Room were opened and the Queen swept in, followed by her two somewhat reluctant companions.

It was when the Deputation had gone and she returned to her apartments that she was informed that the Doctor was waiting to see her.

"Please have him sent to me immediately," the Queen commanded. "And I wish to see him alone!"

The Ladies-in-Waiting, who had joined her when she had left the Throne Room, began to protest.

"It is not correct, Your Majesty!" they said. "Doctor Ansay can attend a lady in the Palace only when there are at least two Ladies-in-Waiting in attendance."

"That may be how it was done in the past," the Queen argued, "but I wish to see the Doctor alone."

She spoke so firmly that there was

nothing the Ladies-in-Waiting could do.

They withdrew as the Doctor came into the room.

As she looked at him, Aldrina felt he was someone she could trust and who would help her.

Doctor Ansay was a man of about fifty, with twinkling eyes and, Aldrina felt, a manner that gave her confidence.

To make sure no one could overhear what they said, she moved across the room to the window which was farthest away from the door.

When the Doctor joined her, she said in a low voice:

"I need your help."

"I am ready to serve Your Majesty in any way I can," he replied.

The Queen gave a little sigh.

Then she said:

"It may seem a strange request, but I want you to prescribe for me a rest away from the Palace and away from the crowd of well-meaning people who seem determined to make me do their bidding twenty-four hours a day."

When she had spoken she held her breath, fearful of his reaction.

The Doctor laughed as if he could not help it, and it was a very comforting sound.

chapter two

"I understand what Your Majesty means," Doctor Ansay said, "and I think I know exactly what you would enjoy."

"What is that?" Aldrina asked a little nervously.

"When His Late Majesty began to be ill," Doctor Ansay explained, "I suggested to him he should go to the seaside. So he had renovated and modernised a house which had been used by one of his relatives until she died."

Aldrina was listening attentively, and he went on:

"It is right on the edge of the sea and a long way from anywhere, for she was a recluse who disliked seeing even her closest friends and relatives."

"That is just what I want at the moment!" Aldrina explained.

"I understand, Ma'am," the Doctor said, "and I shall order you to take a long rest. Perhaps you could start to-morrow or the next day, provided there is no opposition to my prescription."

He smiled as he spoke, and Aldrina

smiled back at him.

"It sounds wonderful!" she said. "And I can really be alone?"

Doctor Ansay shook his head.

"Not entirely alone," he said. "You will have to have a Lady-in-Waiting with you."

"Oh, no!" Aldrina protested. "They talk and talk and never leave me alone for a second."

"They are doing what they believe is their job," the Doctor said. "But I suggest you take the Baroness Fiorilli with you."

Aldrina looked puzzled.

For a moment she could not place the Baroness.

She could see only the two Ladies-in-Waiting who, as she had said, never left her alone.

"Allow me, Ma'am, to tell you about her," the Doctor suggested.

"Please let us sit down," Aldrina said. "I should have asked you to do so before."

The Doctor smiled again.

"His Late Majesty always kept people standing, as I believe your Queen Victoria does," he said. "Some of the older Statesmen complained bitterly that their legs ached, but there was no appeal against His Majesty's ruling."

"It sounds cruel!" Aldrina remarked.

"Please sit down and tell me about the Baroness."

They sat on the sofa, and Doctor Ansay said:

"Baroness Fiorilli was married to a man very much older than herself who, I regret, was cruel and a bully."

Aldrina looked at him in surprise.

"What did he do?" she asked.

"When she had a miscarriage, he beat her, because he had married her in order to beget an heir," the Doctor said quietly. "I attended her afterwards and I told him in no uncertain terms what I thought of him."

"That was brave of you," Aldrina remarked.

"I was protected by the fact that I was Physician to His Late Majesty," Doctor Ansay explained. "But even if he did not beat her again, he certainly made her life a misery. It was, in fact, a merciful release for her when he had a bad fall out riding and broke his neck."

"So the Baroness is a widow like me!" Aldrina remarked.

"It was my suggestion that she should be brought to Court so that she could get away from her husband's relatives, who were almost as aggressive to her as he was.

She is only twenty-six years of age, Ma'am, and she would be a companion for you."

"I am sure she would be," Aldrina agreed. "But the older Ladies-in-Waiting are determined to have my whole attention, and it is difficult for me even to speak to anybody else."

"Then you must certainly have a rest — from them if from no one else!" the Doctor promised.

"That is exactly what I want," Aldrina said, "but please, please, make it very clear that no one is to come with me except the Baroness."

The Doctor thought for a moment.

Then he said:

"You realise, of course, Ma'am, that you must have guards?"

"Oh, no!" Aldrina cried. "I shall feel hedged in and imprisoned."

"Nevertheless," Doctor Ansay said, "if anything should happen to you, I would feel responsible, and I would undoubtedly lose my life."

He gave a short laugh before he said:

"I rather enjoy coming to the Palace, especially now that Your Majesty is on the throne. So permit me to try to arrange to have sent with Your Majesty just four picked guards who in fact are responsible for secret operations which sometimes have to be carried out."

He paused and then continued:

"The officer in command of them is Count Nicolas, a young man whom I would trust with my life, and he would never reveal where you are."

Aldrina drew in her breath.

"That sounds splendid!" she said. "And you mean no one will know where they can find me?"

"It will be a secret from everyone but the Prime Minister," the Doctor agreed. "He needs to be able to get in touch with you in case of any political or diplomatic emergency."

He smiled and continued:

"Otherwise I will try to ensure that you have three weeks of complete freedom from Court protocol and from everyone who wants you to listen to them."

Aldrina clasped her hands together.

"Thank you, thank you!" she exclaimed. "That is exactly what I want. And it will be lovely to be by the sea."

"The house is situated in a very attractive cove," the Doctor explained, "and there is not another house in sight."

"I want to go there at once — this minute!" Aldrina cried.

"I will try to arrange it for to-morrow," the Doctor promised. "I will choose a coachman whom I can trust not to reveal your whereabouts, but I warn you, Ma'am, a great many people will be very inquisitive."

"That is what frightens me," Aldrina replied, "but at least those boring Deputations will not be able to reach me, nor the Privy Council."

"You can leave it in my hands," Doctor Ansay said. "I prescribe a bathe in the sea every day, and sun-bathing when it is not too hot. Then you must go to bed early and dream of all the happiness you hope to have in the future."

Aldrina wondered what that might be.

She did not speak, however, and the Doctor went on:

"Now, Ma'am, I am going to 'put the wheels in motion.' I would like you to talk to the Baroness and tell her exactly what you expect while you two young women are alone in the Fairytale Palace which has never been lived in since His Late Majesty renovated it."

"I shall think of it as my Fairytale Palace," Aldrina said, "and thank you again."

She put out her hand impulsively and added:

"It makes me very happy to know that I have a friend at Court."

Doctor Ansay raised her hand to his lips.

"You are not only very beautiful, Ma'am," he said, "but also very sensible. That is something you will need to be in the years to come."

"I do not want to think about that," Aldrina said. "As you can understand, Doctor, it has been a shock to find myself alone as the Queen of Saria, where I have met not more than a handful of the people."

"The Sarians are very charming people," the Doctor said, "and as I am sure you know, Ma'am, the majority of them are of Greek extraction. There are a few from the other countries around us, but they are very much in the minority."

"I love everything Greek," Aldrina said as she smiled, "and I have dreamt about the Greek gods ever since I was small."

"Then, Ma'am, let us hope you find one." Doctor Ansay smiled.

He rose from the sofa, made a little bow, and walked towards the door.

"Confide in no one," he warned, "and always remember that in this Palace, walls have ears!"

Aldrina laughed.

"I think I have found that out already," she said. "Please, come and see me before I go. I shall want some last-minute instructions from you."

"It will be a great pleasure, Ma'am," the Doctor replied.

When he had gone, Aldrina danced a twirl of excitement.

She had won! She had won!

She was getting away, at least for a short while, from the protocol.

She was escaping from the interminable chatter of her Ladies-in-Waiting and the interminable speeches of the Ministers.

She was also hoping to get away from Prince Inigo.

At luncheon she announced to her two elderly Ladies-in-Waiting that she wanted tea in her private Sitting-Room.

"I wish to be alone," she said, "but I would like to have a few words with Baroness Fiorilli."

The elder of the two Ladies-in-Waiting frowned.

"But, Your Majesty, why do you wish to see the Baroness?" she enquired.

Aldrina did not answer.

She merely said:

"Please see that my wishes are carried out!"

She then walked away.

She was aware that the two ladies looked at each other in consternation, finding this behaviour was something they had not expected.

Aldrina had been overwhelmed by all she had experienced in the short time she had been in Saria.

In consequence she had obediently done everything that was asked of her and had not attempted to assert herself in any way.

When the Baroness Fiorilli came in a little later, Aldrina saw that she was exceedingly pretty.

Her features were classical, she had dark hair and eyes, and a slim, elegant figure.

She made Aldrina a graceful curtsy and said in what was obviously a somewhat nervous manner:

"You wished to see me, Your Majesty?"

"Yes, Baroness," Aldrina replied. "Sit down, I want to talk to you."

The Baroness did as she was told, then said, again in a nervous voice:

"I hope, Ma'am, I have not done anything wrong or to offend you. I have not been in a Palace before, and it is very easy to make mistakes."

"I know that." Aldrina smiled. "Actually,

Baroness, I have been talking to Doctor Ansay."

"He has been very kind to me," the Baroness murmured.

"He told me you are a widow, as I am," Aldrina went on, "and it was at his recommendation that you became a Lady-in-Waiting."

"That is true," the Baroness agreed.

Keeping her voice as low as possible, Aldrina then said:

"I am now going to trust you with a secret, and I know you will not betray me."

"If you trust me, Ma'am," the Baroness said, "I promise I will serve you as faithfully as I can and never do anything you do not wish."

"That is what I hoped you would say," Aldrina answered. "What I want, and what I have arranged with the Doctor, is that you and I shall go away, just the two of us together, to stay at a place he has chosen for us where we can rest undisturbed."

The Baroness stared at Aldrina wide-eyed.

"Alone, Ma'am? But will they let us do that?"

"They will have no choice," Aldrina replied. "The Doctor is arranging it now because I must get away from the eternal

46

chatter of the Palace and the endless speeches I am forced to endure."

The Baroness gave a little laugh.

"I have often felt very sorry for you, Ma'am."

"I am feeling sorry for myself," Aldrina answered, "and the Doctor is going to announce to everybody that it is essential for me to have a complete rest. He will make sure that no one will disturb us while we are away."

"It sounds too marvellous for words," the Baroness murmured, "but I am sure they will try by some means to stop us, Your Majesty."

"The Doctor will say that I must not do anything which he thinks could adversely affect my health," Aldrina answered, "and of course no one must know that you are coming with me. Otherwise the rest of my Ladies-in-Waiting will undoubtedly make a scene."

"They are already protesting to the Prime Minister that I am too young for the post," the Baroness said.

"In which case, I am much too young to be Queen!" Aldrina laughed. "And while we're away I do not wish to be addressed as Ma'am. I will not be the Queen of Saria. I am going to be myself!"

She gave a little laugh as she said:

"Just think of it — no 'Yes, Ma'am. No, Ma'am,' and people being ingratiating. Nobody giving me orders. Nobody except King Neptune, if he cares to come out of the sea to greet me!"

The Baroness laughed.

"You are making it into a Fairy Story, Ma'am," she said.

"That is exactly what it will be," Aldrina said as she smiled, "and, as Doctor Ansay has already said, we are going to a Fairytale Palace, where no one will find us unless, of course, we are joined by the gods from Olympus."

"I think I am dreaming!" the Baroness said. "I have been unhappy for so long that I cannot believe that what you are saying is true!"

"Just wait and see," Aldrina replied. "But remember — not a word to anyone, unless you have a lady's-maid you can trust."

The Baroness shook her head.

"She is also maid to one of the other Ladies-in-Waiting," she said, "and is therefore a terrible gossip."

"Then we will just have to take mine with us," Aldrina said. "She is English and came with me from England, chosen by my mother."

48

"Then you can trust her?" the Baroness questioned.

"I can, because she is already devoted to me," Aldrina answered. "Moreover, she does not speak any language but English. She has no idea what the people around her are talking about, although I am teaching her a little Greek just to make it easier for her to order whatever I require."

"Every word you say, Ma'am, makes me feel that this is going to be an exciting adventure for us both."

"That is what I am sure it will be," Aldrina replied. "Now I suggest, Baroness, that you go and pack your own things, but do not let anyone know or suspect that you are leaving the Palace."

"I will do that, Ma'am, and thank you, thank you!" the Baroness said.

She rose from where she had been sitting, curtsied to Aldrina, then said in a broken voice:

"You are so . . . kind to me . . . that I . . . feel . . . I want . . . to cry."

Before Aldrina could say anything, the Baroness had gone from the room.

No sooner had she disappeared than the two elderly Ladies-in-Waiting came bustling in.

"I am sure now that you have finished

with the Baroness, Ma'am, you require us," one of them said.

"Actually," Aldrina replied, "I am going to write a letter to my mother, and you will understand that I would find other people in the room somewhat distracting. If I need you later, I will send someone to summon you. Otherwise, we will meet again at dinner."

The Ladies-in-Waiting were dismissed and looked somewhat disgruntled as they left the room.

Aldrina went to the writing-desk and sat down to write a long letter to her mother.

She wrote to her almost every day, knowing that she would be eager to hear every detail of what was happening in Saria.

She had been unable to accompany her daughter as she had wished to do because she suffered a great deal from asthma.

The Doctors had therefore advised against the long journey which would be detrimental to her health.

Aldrina had thought privately that this was just an excuse to make her go alone with the Ambassador and his wife, and the Ladies-in-Waiting.

"I want you to come with me, Mama!" she had said over and over again.

But her mother had said:

"If I go against the Doctors' orders and the Ambassador's advice, darling, and anything happens to me on the voyage, they might be blamed."

She sighed and then continued:

"I hate the idea of your going alone, and I shall be thinking of you every moment. But I feel in this case we must obey the instructions which have come not only from Saria, but also from Her Majesty the Queen."

"Queen Victoria never bothered about us until now," Aldrina pointed out.

Her mother knew this was true.

Although she did not say so, she thought that Aldrina would not have been sent to Saria if there had been anybody else available.

Queen Victoria was known as the "Matchmaker of Europe," and she had put members of her family and of the Prince Consort's into every possible country.

In fact, there were already over twenty crowned heads who were in some way connected with the British Royal Family.

Queen Victoria was not particularly generous to those dependent on her who were not of great importance.

Princess Adelaide, Aldrina's mother, was

the daughter of a very distant relative of the Queen's mother, the Duchess of Kent.

She had married because she had fallen in love with Prince Ferdinand, who reigned over a small Aegean island.

He had lost his throne when it was annexed to Greece.

They had come to England because it was his wife's country.

Almost immediately after their arrival, he died from appendicitis, which the Doctors did not know how to treat.

Princess Adelaide was broken-hearted at her loss.

She was also penniless.

None of her own family had enough means to look after her and her young daughter.

A desperate appeal to the Queen gave her a Grace and Favour apartment in Hampton Court Palace; also, a very small allowance was granted on which to live.

Every penny had to be carefully considered before they actually spent it.

Aldrina could not help thinking that if her mother had been allowed to come with her, at least she could have enjoyed the excellent food that was provided at the Palace.

The wine which was served to the members of the Household would have done her good, as would the comfort in which everybody lived.

The Princess would have had servants to look after her like everybody else in the Palace.

"I am sure," Aldrina told herself, "I should have made more fuss about coming alone and insisted on Mama coming with me."

She quickly determined to send her mother money so that she could be much more comfortable than she had ever been in the past.

She had already spoken to the Chancellor of the Exchequer, saying to him:

"I would like to know, Chancellor, exactly what money I myself have to spend, although I know it is correct for Royalty not to carry any themselves."

The Chancellor of the Exchequer smiled.

"That is true, Ma'am, and of course you may buy anything you require. If you want hard cash at any time, you have only to ask your Private Secretary, who will give you what you need."

"My Private Secretary?" Aldrina exclaimed. "I had no idea I had one!"

"But of course you have, Ma'am!" the

Chancellor answered. "He answers a great number of letters with which there is no need to trouble you, and organises your engagements!"

Aldrina sent for her Private Secretary the very next morning.

She was not surprised to find that he was an elderly man who had been at the Palace for many years.

She did not "beat about the bush," but came straight to the point, saying to him firmly:

"I wish to give my mother in England a regular allowance. She is very poor and I want her to be comfortable. Can you arrange it?"

"Certainly, Your Majesty, if you will tell me how much you wish her to have."

Aldrina named a sum which seemed to her enormous.

Her Secretary, however, did not flicker an eyelid.

"I will have that amount transferred regularly to the Bank of Your Majesty's mother, if Ma'am will be so kind as to tell me the name."

Aldrina told him and had run to her room later to write to her mother and tell her the good news.

'That, at least, is one advantage of being

a Queen!' she thought. 'But there are certainly quite a number of disadvantages.'

She was thinking of her chattering Ladies-in-Waiting, and, because he was never far from her thoughts, Prince Inigo.

It was almost as though she had summoned him by just thinking of him.

A servant opened the door and announced:

"His Royal Highness the Prince Inigo requests an audience with Your Majesty."

As the Prince came into the room, Aldrina said:

"I am very busy, Your Royal Highness. I am writing to my mother and have no time to see anyone."

"I will not keep you long," the Prince said. "I merely came to tell you that I am deeply perturbed to hear that you are not well. I understand you saw the Doctor this afternoon."

It flashed through Aldrina's mind that his spies, whom he undoubtedly had in the Palace, had not wasted much time in communicating with him.

She rose from the desk to say:

"To be honest, I am feeling rather tired and, naturally, upset at His Majesty's death. It was not what I expected when I left England to come to Saria."

"A voyage you should not have been forced to make!" the Prince said disagreeably.

Then, as if he remembered that he was trying to woo her, he added quickly:

"Of course we were extremely fortunate in having anyone so lovely and so charming to come to be our Queen."

He put down a bouquet of flowers he was carrying on one of the tables and said:

"Surely, Aldrina, you realise by this time how much you mean to me?"

"I have not given you permission to address me by my Christian name!" Aldrina retorted.

"As we are so nearly related," Prince Inigo said, "you can hardly expect me to call you 'Your Majesty,' or 'Ma'am,' every half-second! And my name is Inigo."

"I am aware of that," Aldrina said, "but I prefer to know people well before I become so familiar."

"I want you to know me very well," the Prince replied, "and what I have come to suggest is that you might like to come and stay at my Palace in the country for a week or so. My mother would be delighted to have you. It would be a change of air for you, and I can understand that the Funeral has been upsetting for you."

"It is a very kind thought," Aldrina said.

She was thinking quickly as she went on:

"I will, of course, consider it carefully, but there is a great deal for me to do here."

"It can wait until you return," the Prince said. "May I tell my mother that you will come to us the day after to-morrow? It is only two hours' drive from here. I promise you will be very comfortable and I will try to amuse you in every way I can."

"That is very considerate of you," Aldrina replied, "but as I have said, I need time to think it over and of course to consult Doctor Ansay, who is prescribing for me."

"If you ask me, there is nothing wrong with you but a slight depression," the Prince said. "All this mourning is enough to depress anyone! I will arrange a dance for you when you come to my home."

"A dance?" Aldrina exclaimed. "But surely Your Royal Highness realises that the whole country would be shocked at the idea of my dancing so soon after my husband's death?"

"Those old fuddy-duddies in the Government would be shocked," the Prince said. "They are shocked at anything! We will just have a few of my friends, who will be asked to keep the party a secret, and perhaps I can get a Gypsy Band to play for us. It will make you feel very romantic."

He looked at her as he spoke in a way which told her he wanted her to feel romantic with him.

She knew it was the last thing she was ever likely to do.

She was sure that if she accepted his invitation and went to his Palace, he would try to make love to her.

That would be extremely embarrassing and to escape would be difficult.

"Thank you for thinking of me," she said, "but now, if you please, I must finish my letter to my mother."

The Prince moved a little nearer to her.

"I do not intend to take 'No' for an answer, on this or on any other matter," he said in a low voice.

Aldrina had the sudden thought that he was about to put his arms around her.

She moved quickly back to her chair in front of the writing-desk and picked up her pen.

"Thank you for the flowers," she said, "and now I really must finish this letter."

She bent her head and started to write on the heavily embossed paper.

The Prince hesitated.

Aldrina knew perceptively that he was

wondering whether he dared pull her to her feet and force her to promise she would stay with him at his Palace.

Then, as if he realised that to do so might precipitate a crisis to his disadvantage, he walked towards the door.

"I will be waiting to hear what day you have decided to come and stay at my home," he said.

There was a note of anger in his voice.

He was obviously resenting the way she was getting rid of him.

As he left the room she gave a sigh of relief.

He had gone.

Now she could concentrate on the letter to her mother.

She was thinking that after to-morrow she would be free of the Prince until she returned.

She knew it was foolish to be frightened of him.

Yet she could feel vibrating from him his determination to make her his wife and thereby to rule over Saria.

Ever since she had been a child, Aldrina had been perceptive about the people she met.

"I can feel what they are like inside, Mama," she had said to her mother.

The Princess had understood.

"Before you were born, dearest," she said, "I was told by a Gypsy that I would have a daughter who would be famous and reign in a far-off country. She also said she would be 'blessed by the stars,' and they would show her all her life what was right and what was wrong."

"Is that really true, Mama?" Aldrina had asked.

"I think you must find that out for yourself," the Princess replied. "But remember, when you are making a decision, the stars will help you. That means, my darling, that if you pray, you will find the right answer."

Aldrina knew now that the stars were telling her quite clearly that Prince Inigo was a dangerous if not evil man.

She must beware of him.

It was certainly very difficult in the Palace to keep him away.

She could only pray that he would not find out by some means of his own where she was going.

Then she told herself she must trust Doctor Ansay.

'I am very lucky to have him,' she thought.

She felt it was actually the stars that were guiding her now and she need not be afraid.

She finished the letter she was sending to her mother, giving her all her love.

She ended the page with kisses, then added a "P. S." which said:

"As soon as possible, dearest Mama, you must come and stay here. I am sure I can arrange it when I come back from my holiday, and if there is any difficulty about it affecting your asthma, I will send Doctor Ansay to travel with you."

She had only just thought of this, and when she had written it she looked out of the window at the sky.

There were no stars to be seen.

The sun was shining and the sky was a clear blue.

"I am a Queen," she said, "and as a Queen I can do things I never thought possible. I am sure it is all due to you."

She was speaking to the stars, although she could not see them.

But she felt they were near her, caring for her, protecting her, and at the same time inspiring her.

"Help me," she begged softly, "for no one but you can protect me against the Prince."

Even as she spoke she felt as if he had

left his vibrations behind him.

They were still there in the room, menacing her, making it impossible to forget that he intended by one means or another to marry her.

She gave a little shiver before she rang the bell for a servant to come and take to her Secretary the letter addressed to her mother.

He would ensure that it was sent by the quickest route to England.

As she waited for the door to open, she looked again at the sky.

"I am not . . . really afraid," she said firmly.

At the same time, she knew that was not true.

chapter three

As soon as she saw the Fairytale Palace, Aldrina knew it was exactly what she wanted.

It was a long, low building set on high ground just above the Cove with a path sloping down to the Sea.

It was backed by trees which protected it from the winds and, painted white, it glittered like a jewel.

As they drove towards it, Aldrina said to the Baroness:

"We have won! We have won! No one knows where we are, and we can spend three weeks just enjoying ourselves!"

"It is very exciting for me," the Baroness replied.

Aldrina walked into the house and found it was beautifully furnished.

There was furniture carved and painted by the locals and rugs in brilliant colours made by the Greeks.

They glowed against the white walls and the sofas and chairs which were mostly covered in white.

It would be cool in the house all the Summer.

The huge windows could be shut on cooler days so that one could see the view while keeping out the wind.

The garden, to Aldrina's joy, was filled with Spring flowers.

She and the Baroness had crept away from the Palace very early so that no one would know they had gone until much later.

It was Doctor Ansay's idea.

They went out through a back door, where a carriage he had ordered was waiting for them.

Behind it was a Brake carrying the guards and Aldrina's lady's-maid.

Aldrina noticed that as they made their way to the sea, the guards kept well back so as not to intrude on them.

She hoped they would do the same when they arrived at their destination.

Doctor Ansay had told her that they would be living in the Guard House, where they could look after themselves.

She need have no contact with them, but could be assured that they would keep her safe and would exclude intruders.

"In actual fact you will have no visitors," Doctor Ansay said. "The house has not been open for years, and I do not think you have many neighbours."

"That is exactly what I want," Aldrina replied, "and thank you again for being so kind."

They had managed to drive away from the Palace without being seen.

Aldrina told herself she was very lucky to have such a good friend.

She thought she would promote him in some way when she returned to the City and resumed her duties as Queen.

She had been thinking about it on the journey down.

Now, as she looked round the pretty Sitting-Room, she said to the Baroness:

"This is what I have decided: From this moment I cease to be the Queen and you cease to be my Lady-in-Waiting. I shall call you Sophie, which I know is your Christian name, and you will call me . . ."

She hesitated for a moment before she said:

". . . not Aldrina, because anyone hearing it might associate it with the Queen of Saria. No, you must call me 'Drina,' which is the name I called myself when I was a child because I could not pronounce my whole name."

Sophie laughed.

"I told you we were stepping into a Fairy Story, and this makes it even more exciting."

"Of course it does!" Aldrina agreed. "And you may do anything you wish to do, with no one to reprimand you for it, or say you should be doing something else."

She swung out her full skirts as she danced around, then sank down on one of the white-covered sofas.

"Now — what shall we do?" she asked.

Sophie hesitated for a moment, then she said:

"The sea will not be cold. Why do we not bathe in it?"

"An excellent suggestion, and that is what we will do," Aldrina said, approving of the idea.

She would have run up the stairs, but she found there were servants waiting in the hall to speak to her.

There was an elderly couple who Doctor Ansay had told her would be there because they had been looking after the house.

With them was a younger man who she thought must be the Chef, and a country girl who was obviously the housemaid.

She found when she spoke to them that they spoke only the language of their country.

It was near enough to Greek for Aldrina to understand what they were saying.

At the same time, she thought with joy

66

that long conversations would be impossible.

The older woman curtsied and asked her if she would like anything to eat or drink.

Aldrina told her to put something on the table for when they came downstairs.

The bed-rooms were delightful, all with huge windows overlooking the sea.

There were large, comfortable beds which could easily have held three or four people.

Her lady's-maid was already unpacking in the largest bed-room, and Aldrina said to her:

"I hope you will be comfortable, Lucy. I am afraid you will not be able to communicate with these servants, so you must tell me if there is anything you want."

"That'll be all right, Ma'am," Lucy replied. "I'll make them do what I want!"

Aldrina had already spoken to her about being careful not to let anybody know who she was.

She thought it was a blessing in disguise that there would be no chattering in the Servants' Hall.

There would be no whispering of secrets such as she was sure took place in the Palace.

She carefully took off the gown in which

she had travelled and put on her bathing-dress.

Fortunately she had brought one with her from England.

After she and Sophie had had some delicious fruit-juice to drink they ran out into the garden, hand-in-hand.

They followed a path which led them to the Cove.

The sand was golden and there were few stones.

The sea was calm, with no more than ripples on the surface, while the sun dazzled with a golden glow.

Aldrina had learnt to swim when her mother had taken her to the seaside.

The sea was much warmer than it had been in England, and Aldrina swam out a long way before she turned to look back.

The view was entrancing.

She felt really happy for the first time since she had come to Saria.

"I am happy! I am happy!" she wanted to call to the gulls.

Sophie, who was not so strong a swimmer, joined her.

"I will race you!" Aldrina said after they had talked for some minutes.

They swam back to the shore, Aldrina beating Sophie by two lengths.

Despite the fact that there were no Deputations and no Privy Council to lecture her, Aldrina was quite tired by dinner-time.

As soon as the meal, which was simple but delicious, was over, she told Sophie she was going to bed.

"To be honest," she explained, "I have not slept very well since coming to Saria. There have been so many things to worry about."

She thought as she spoke that one of them had been Prince Inigo.

She was praying that when he learnt she had disappeared he would not discover where she had gone.

She was quite certain he would try to find her.

She could imagine nothing more infuriating than for him to turn up.

He would start paying her the usual insincere compliments, and would try to force her into saying she would marry him.

"I will not think about him," she told herself when she got into bed.

But it was difficult not to wonder what she could do when she returned to the Palace.

How could she stop him from intruding on her?

However, she was even more tired than she thought, for she fell asleep almost immediately.

Aldrina did not stir until the rays of the rising sun came peeping through the curtains.

She woke to find that it was just after dawn.

In fact, it was five o'clock in the morning.

She felt well and excited, having slept for quite a time, and jumped out of bed.

Pulling back the curtains, she decided she would go down to the beach.

She decided not to wake Sophie because she really wanted to be on her own.

She liked being alone.

Because her mother could never afford to have a full-time Governess for her, she had wandered about Hampton Court Palace by herself.

Sometimes she would walk along the bank of the Thames, watching the boats pass by and the swans swimming in the shallow water.

When she got downstairs she realised it was too early for any of the servants to be awake.

She let herself out through one of the Drawing-Room windows, and ran across the garden and down to the Cove.

She thought it would be fun to go farther along the coast.

She wanted to explore the unknown territory that surrounded the house.

She walked barefoot along the sand, finding it warm on her bare feet.

There was a faint morning breeze to play in her hair.

She walked for some distance.

The birds were nesting in the cliffs above her.

She listened to the sound of the small waves as they gently rolled in and out from the smooth sea.

Then, just ahead, she saw a boat sailing towards the shore.

A very attractive craft with two red sails, it was moving slowly because there was very little wind.

The man who was navigating it had to keep changing direction to catch what breeze there was to take it to the shore.

It was then Aldrina realised that the smaller sail had become detached.

She understood that it was difficult for the man to manoeuvre the boat as well as he might otherwise have done.

There was just enough wind to bring him to the beach.

The boat ran up onto the sand just as Aldrina reached it.

The sailor stepped out into the shallow water and instinctively she began to help him pull his boat up onto the sand.

It was what she had often done when she had been at the seaside with her mother.

The boatmen had taken her out when they were not otherwise employed and taught her how to sail a boat by adjusting the sails.

Then they had taught her how to navigate.

Now, as the man finished pulling the boat up to safety, she looked at him and realised he was very good looking.

In fact, he was very different from the boatmen she had known at the seaside in England.

He was dark-haired and had the dark eyes of a Greek.

His features were clear-cut, and he was extremely handsome.

It flashed through her mind that he might be one of the Greek gods.

He looked at her and said in Greek:

"Thank you — I did not expect a Goddess to help me!"

Aldrina laughed and said:

"I was just wondering if you had

dropped down from Olympus!"

The man's eyes twinkled.

"If I had, I am quite certain I should already have met you there! But what can you be doing in this isolated spot?"

He sounded so surprised that Aldrina replied:

"I have just arrived to stay in the only house that seems to exist on this part of the coast."

"Are you telling me that you're staying in the white Villa which is about half-a-mile to our left?" the man asked.

Aldrina nodded.

"Good heavens!" he exclaimed. "I had no idea that anyone lived there except for an old couple whom I have sometimes seen sitting in the Cove in the evenings."

Aldrina thought quickly. Then she said:

"My friend and I have rented it for a few weeks."

The man smiled.

"What is your friend doing at the moment? Can it be possible he is sleeping on such a lovely morning?"

"That is exactly what *she* is doing!" Aldrina replied, emphasising the pronoun. "But, like you, I thought it was too lovely to be wasted."

"I always enjoy it here at this time of the

day when there is nobody about," the man said. "I like to think I am 'Master of all I survey.' "

Aldrina laughed again.

"You are certainly that. The sea was completely empty until you appeared."

"And now, what shall we do about it?" the man enquired.

There was a look in his eyes that Aldrina found exciting.

She could not help feeling it was delightful to be able to talk to someone without their bowing and calling her "Ma'am," or "Your Majesty" every other second.

"I suppose," she said, "you ought to repair your sail which I see has become detached."

"That will not take me long," the man said, "and I would like you to help me, in payment for which I will take you out to sea."

"I would enjoy that," Aldrina said quickly. "I love sailing, but I have never been in such a beautiful vessel."

"I accept the compliment with delight," the man said, "for the simple reason that I myself designed the *Sea Maiden*, and now that I think about it — I must have realised it was an aptly named boat for you."

Aldrina chuckled.

The man reached out towards the small red sail which had become detached.

As he started to mend it he said:

"Suppose you tell me your name, unless, of course, it is Aphrodite?"

"I only wish it were," Aldrina replied. "Actually it is Drina."

She thought as she spoke she was perfectly safe in telling him that.

He would never for a moment connect the name with Queen Aldrina of Saria.

"A pretty name," he said, "but I think I shall call you Aphrodite, after the Goddess who has caused more trouble in the world than all the other Goddesses put together!"

"I am sure that is not the right thing to say!" Aldrina protested. "After all, everyone wants love, and without it the world would be a very dull and dreary place."

She was thinking, as she spoke, of the dreams she had on her way to Saria.

She had thought that the man she was to marry, because he was partly Greek, would look very like the stranger who was talking to her now.

She had been filled with dismay when she had seen the King, old and bald, lying against the white linen pillows.

"You are looking unhappy," the man said. "What has upset you?"

"It is only something in the past," Aldrina replied, "and it cannot upset me anymore, so I shall try to stop myself from thinking about it."

"That is very sensible," the man said approvingly.

"Instead of talking about me," Aldrina went on, "let us talk about you. What is your name?"

"It is Juro," he said without a moment's pause. "But I am quite content to be Apollo if you prefer."

"The God of Light," Aldrina remembered aloud. "Is that what you are bringing to the world?"

"I wish I could answer that question more fully," Juro answered. "But shall I say that I love light, and I like people with light in their eyes — like you!"

He studied her for a moment before he said suddenly:

"You are not Greek."

"I am English," Aldrina explained, "but I have some Greek blood in my veins."

"That is what deceived me," Juro said, and he spoke in English.

Aldrina gave a little cry of surprise.

"You speak English!"

"Why should you be so surprised?" he enquired. "I have been well-educated, and I have many English friends."

He spoke a little aggressively, and Aldrina said:

"I . . . I am sorry . . . I did not mean to sound insulting . . . but it has been a long time since I have met someone who speaks my language."

As she spoke, Aldrina thought it was really only a short time.

So much had happened, however, since she had left her mother at Hampton Court Palace to come to Saria, that she felt as if she had lived through a century of disappointments, surprises, and fear.

"Now you are looking worried again," Juro said observantly. "You told me you would be sensible and forget the past."

"That is what I am trying to do."

"You are not trying hard enough," he said. "When I feel worried I shut my emotions off and tell them to behave themselves, and they do as they are told."

"What you have just said tells me that we have some thoughts in common."

Juro laughed, and she knew he was well aware that she was hiding something from him.

She did not ask herself how she knew

that was what he was thinking.

He seemed a very easy person to talk to.

She thought, as he worked on the sail, that she had never seen a more handsome man.

He was wearing just a white shirt with short sleeves, and shorts like men wore for football.

His skin was tanned by the sun so that it was honey-coloured.

His square shoulders and narrow hips were those of an athlete.

Having mended the sail, he now said:

"Come along. As you helped me pull the *Sea Maiden* onto the sand, you must now help me push her out."

Aldrina did as she was told, and when the boat was afloat, Juro, without any warning, picked her up and lifted her into it.

As he did so, she realised how strong he was.

He took his place at the tiller and said:

"You are as light as thistledown. Are you quite certain you will not fly away from me?"

"I will try not to," Aldrina said as she smiled, "but, of course, you will have to be very polite and kind, for otherwise I can always swim away."

"I can think of quite a number of things I can be besides 'polite and kind,' " Juro remarked, "but perhaps on such short acquaintance I had better keep them to myself."

Aldrina knew he was paying her a compliment.

At the same time, as she could read his thoughts, she blushed.

Juro stared at her.

"It is a long time since I have seen a woman blush," he said. "I hope it is something you do often, for I find it absolutely entrancing!"

"You are . . . making me feel . . . shy," Aldrina murmured.

"I find that even more attractive," he said. "Women in every part of the world are becoming less shy and more aggressive, and if you have ever met any of the new breed, you will know exactly what I am saying."

"I expect, like all men, you want a woman to be soft and pliable, and ready to obey your every whim!" Aldrina teased.

"It is certainly an idea, but one which is difficult to find in practice," Juro answered.

Aldrina thought that because he was so exceedingly masculine and strong, most women would be only too glad to obey him.

At the same time, she felt in a way she could not explain that he was trustworthy and kind.

They sailed a long way out to sea.

In fact, when Aldrina looked back, the Fairytale Palace was only a tiny white dot on a long, empty coast.

Doctor Ansay had been right.

There really were no other houses in sight except for some far away to the right, where she saw the River Leeka pouring into the sea. On the other side of the river could be seen a number of spires and towers silhouetted against the sky.

Juro, following the direction of her eyes, said:

"You are looking at Xanthe, which is an unpleasant country filled with people I think you would find unpleasant too."

"What is wrong with them?" Aldrina enquired.

He shrugged his shoulders.

"They are set a bad example by their Rulers, and a number of ne'er-do-wells from other countries have moved there so that they can practise their nefarious activities uninterrupted."

Aldrina did not answer.

80

She thought it would be a mistake to admit she knew of Prince Terome, and that he was said to be an unpleasant young man.

She thought, however, he could not be more repulsive than Prince Inigo.

She realised that in every country there were good and bad, and one had to choose between them.

"Exactly!" Juro said. "But I prefer them to be good, like you."

Aldrina looked at him in astonishment.

"How can you read my thoughts?"

"In the same way that you have been reading mine," he answered. "I admit it is strange, but your eyes are as expressive as your lips."

He looked at her mouth, and once again Aldrina blushed.

It struck her that she was behaving in a very reprehensible fashion, going sailing with a young man she had only just met.

And, of course, without a chaperon.

"I . . . I think I ought to . . . go back," she said a little hesitatingly.

Juro put out his hand and laid it on hers.

"Forgive me," he said pleadingly. "I find it very hard not to make you blush because you do it so exquisitely, but I do not want you to be afraid of me."

"I am not," Aldrina said without thinking. "It . . . is just that I . . . I suddenly realised I . . . should be chaperoned."

Juro put back his head and laughed aloud. "How can you think of anything so ridiculous, here in a world where there is no one but ourselves? I am sure you had no chaperons on Mount Olympus!"

Aldrina had to agree that what she had said was ridiculous.

At the same time, she could never remember being alone with a young man in a boat, or anywhere else, and able to talk to him so frankly and freely.

"What we have to do," Juro said, "is to thank the gods for introducing us to each other. Or, rather, for damaging my sail so that I had to bring the boat ashore in order to put it right."

"You thank the gods for that?" Aldrina asked.

"Who else?" he enquired. "They wanted us to meet and we have met. Surely you're not going to argue about that?"

"I am not going to argue," she said, "because I think it is very wonderful. At the same time, I do not want you to think I intruded on your solitude."

"Now you are fishing for compliments,"

Juro said. "Let me tell you, I was, in fact, feeling rather lonely and thinking I would like to share the beauty of the dawn with somebody who would understand."

"I . . . I think I do understand," Aldrina said.

Juro thought for a moment before he replied:

"If we think in the right way, then the world is an enchanting place where miracles do happen."

He looked at Aldrina as he spoke.

She knew he was telling her he thought it was a miracle that they had met, and it was what she was thinking herself.

After a moment he asked in a different voice:

"Have you really got to go back?"

"Yes, but there is no particular hurry," Aldrina replied. "My friend will guess that I have gone down to the shore, but she may want to stay in bed because, like me, she was very tired last night."

"Where have you come from?" Juro asked.

"The . . . City," Aldrina replied.

"Is your friend English, like you?"

Aldrina shook her head.

"No, she is from Saria, and very sweet and gentle. She has had a very unhappy marriage, so she wanted to get away and forget everything that is a reminder of the past."

"And you felt the same?" Juro said. "Very well, we will pretend that your life started to-day, when you and I met, and we will both of us forget anything that happened before that moment when you helped me to pull the boat ashore."

"Do you . . . really believe we can . . . do that?" Aldrina asked seriously.

"Of course we can," he said. "Nothing is of any importance except that we should enjoy ourselves, and do not waste time in thinking about what happened yesterday, or what is going to happen to-morrow."

His eyes twinkled as he added:

"Or what people will say, which is the least important thing of all!"

"I . . . I suppose you are right," Aldrina conceded not very confidently.

"If you listen to all the criticisms made by people who are jealous, you will only be miserable," Juro said. "Now, forget everything and tell me if you like Saria better than England."

"It is difficult to compare the two," Aldrina said. "They are so completely different, but I want to be happy in Saria."

"You are going to stay there?"

She nodded.

"Then stay and try to enjoy yourself, just as the people of Saria will enjoy you," Juro said.

He turned the boat into the wind before he asked:

"How can you be so incredibly lovely, and at the same time real?"

He spoke in an ordinary voice that did not make it seem embarrassing, and Aldrina replied quickly:

"How can you look like a Greek god . . . unless you are one?"

Juro looked at her, and suddenly they both laughed.

"Are we really having this conversation?" he asked.

"It certainly seems strange, when we have only just met," Aldrina answered. "But I enjoy talking to you, and I suppose it would be wrong and . . . incorrect for me to ask you if you would . . . like to come back for breakfast?"

"That is a very sensible suggestion," Juro said as he smiled, "and now that I come to think of it, I am feeling hungry."

He turned the boat as he spoke.

There was enough wind now to carry the boat safely into the Cove.

He did not speak as he manoeuvred the

boat, and as the sails suddenly flopped down, Juro got out into the water to pull the boat up on the beach.

As Aldrina joined him, she remembered she had not had her bathe in the sea, but that was something she would do after luncheon.

She could not help feeling apprehensive as, having pulled the boat on to the sand, they climbed up the twisting path which led towards the Villa's garden.

'Perhaps I have made a mistake,' Aldrina thought. 'Perhaps I should have said goodbye and just hoped I would meet him another day.'

Then she knew she wanted Juro to stay with her for as long as possible.

She was frightened that perhaps if he sailed away she would never see him again.

'Sophie will think it strange,' she thought as they walked up the path together.

Quite suddenly Juro stopped.

"No!" he said.

"No?" Aldrina enquired.

"This is a mistake," he explained. "Something strange and wonderful has happened this morning. You came to me from the sea, and that is where you belong. It would be a mistake for us to go back now to reality."

Aldrina could think of nothing to say; she could only stare at him, her eyes very wide.

Then he said:

"I will wait for you on the beach to-morrow morning at the same time."

With that, he walked quickly away, and she watched him go in astonishment.

She thought he would turn and perhaps wave, but he went on until he was only a dot in the distance.

It was then she walked slowly up the path and into the Villa.

chapter four

There was no one about and Aldrina realised it was still early.

She sat down in a chair and tried to collect her thoughts and think of what had happened that morning.

Some time later the man-servant appeared, and seeing her there went back to the kitchen.

She knew he had gone to fetch her breakfast, and she went into the Dining-Room.

She breakfasted alone, because there was no sign of Sophie.

In fact, she did not appear until midday.

By this time Aldrina was lying on the balcony in a comfortable chair, her feet raised and with the sun-blind pulled out over her head.

The sun was dazzling on the sea which was as blue as the Madonna's robe.

Aldrina could not help hoping she would see a red sail moving along the coast.

Except for a couple of cargo boats, however, there was nothing to vary the emptiness and the brilliance.

"Forgive me! Forgive me!" Sophie said as she came to Aldrina's side. "I have never slept quite so late in my life!"

"I am sure it is what you needed to do," Aldrina answered.

Sophie sat down in a chair beside her.

"I have not slept without waking in the night since my husband died," she answered. "I was made so miserable by his relatives, who were angry that he had married me and begrudged me every penny that I had been left in his Will."

"Forget them!" Aldrina said.

"That is what I am trying to do," Sophie agreed, "and to-day, after my long sleep, I feel quite different. When I was in the Palace I kept waking up thinking somebody was calling me."

"There is only me to call you now," Aldrina said, "and I too slept very well."

As she spoke, she decided she would not tell Sophie what had happened that morning.

Somehow she did not want to talk about it, and anyway, it would be hard to explain how she had made the acquaintance of a man she had never seen before, or that she had gone sailing with him.

In fact, it had been so much more than that, but something she could not put into words.

She knew that Juro was right when he said it would be a mistake to step back into reality.

"I shall see him to-morrow," Aldrina told herself not once, but a hundred times during the day.

She and Sophie swam in the sea, and the only person they saw was Count Nicolas, the officer in charge of their guards, who came in merely to see if there was anything they wanted.

"We have peace, which is all we really need," Aldrina told him with a smile.

He was an attractive young man of about twenty-eight, and she was sure his ancestry was Greek.

"I just wondered," he said, "if, Ma'am, you would like some newspapers, or anything else that you do not have at the moment."

He paused and then continued:

"There is a small village about three miles away, and it would not take me or one of my men long to ride there and buy anything you required."

"Speaking for myself," Aldrina said, "I want nothing more than I have already."

"I can say the same," Sophie added in a soft voice.

The Count saluted and left them.

"He seems a very tactful man," Aldrina said when he had gone, "and Doctor Ansay assured me that I could trust him with my life."

"I am sure that is true," Sophie agreed. "It is reassuring to know we are safe and well protected, and that no one can burst in upon us when we least expect it."

"Safe — for three weeks!" Aldrina said with satisfaction.

They had dinner early because after so much exercise they wanted to go to bed.

Aldrina felt guilty at being so eager to do so because she knew she would be getting up very early the next morning.

But she still thought it would be a mistake to tell Sophie what she had done.

Sophie had told her a little about herself during the afternoon, and Aldrina learned what a terrible life she had led with a husband who had treated her so brutally.

"Why did you marry him?" she asked.

"My father and mother thought it was a very good match because he was a Baron and, of course, very rich."

She paused and then continued:

"He saw me at a Ball that was given by some neighbours, and although I was frightened of him because he was so much older than I was, I thought that Papa and

91

Mama knew best when they told me I was to marry him."

"But you were not in love," Aldrina said quietly.

"No, of course not," Sophie declared. "I had hardly seen my husband until we were actually married, as the rules are very strict here about a man and an unmarried girl being alone together."

Aldrina felt a little twinge of conscience as she remembered how she had been alone with Juro all the morning.

Then she told herself that she was not an unmarried girl, but a widow.

She had taken off her wedding-ring to go swimming because it was a little loose, and she thought it might slip off when her fingers were cold.

She had not, however, put it on again when she dressed.

Lying in bed with the moonlight coming through the window, she told herself that she would not wear it while she was here.

It might seem reprehensible, but she had no wish for Juro to ask her questions.

"He must never know I am a Queen," she said. "Otherwise I am certain he will treat me with propriety, bowing and saying 'Ma'am' after every word."

She felt a little thrill run through her as

she thought how exciting it had been to be able to talk to him as if she were just an ordinary girl.

Then she remembered that they did not think of each other as "ordinary," but as part of the gods, the God of Light and the Goddess of Love.

She was sure Juro looked exactly as Apollo must have looked when he drove his chariot across the sky or arriving at Delphi on the back of a dolphin.

It was there that he had looked up at the "shining cliffs" and claimed for himself all the land beneath them.

She could imagine Juro doing just that.

Then she laughed at her fantasy because she was making him part of a Fairytale that had been hers ever since she had come to the Fairytale Palace by the sea.

'If I over-sleep he will go away without me,' she thought as she shut her eyes.

As if her will-power acted like an alarm, Aldrina awoke as soon as dawn broke in the sky.

The rising sun was sweeping away the last of the stars.

She jumped out of bed and put on her bathing-dress.

Her mother had made it for her when

they had been at the seaside in England, and it was of a white material that did not cling too closely to her body.

It was very modest, having short sleeves and a full skirt.

She knew that in England the Ladies of Quality who bathed at Brighton or any of the other fashionable resorts would have worn stockings.

She wondered if Juro was perhaps shocked that her legs were bare.

Then she told herself that the way he was dressed was hardly formal, and she would look ridiculous walking over the sand in stockings.

Just as she had done the previous day, she slipped out of the house through the French window in the Drawing-Room.

She ran down the path which led to the beach, but as she hurried along she thought that perhaps, as she was so early, he would not yet be there.

On the other hand, he might have changed his mind and found something better to do.

Then, when she was still a little way from where he had beached his boat the previous day, she saw him approaching.

There was no mistaking the bright red sails and, as there was a dawn wind, he was moving quickly.

By the time Aldrina reached their meeting-place, he was there.

He navigated his boat as near to the shore as he could.

Then she walked through the shallow water towards him, and he bent and lifted her into the boat.

"I was afraid you might have forgotten," he said as he did so.

"I thought you could have a more important engagement," Aldrina replied.

He laughed.

"What could be more important than a rendezvous with Aphrodite?" he enquired. "And may I tell you that you are looking very lovely this morning?"

Because the compliment was unexpected, Aldrina blushed.

Juro watched the darkening colour in her cheeks.

Then he said:

"You look like the dawn itself, and I had forgotten that a woman could look so lovely when she is shy."

Feeling a little embarrassed, Aldrina turned her face away from him.

"Where are we going?" she asked.

"Out to sea," Juro replied, "and as that is where you came from, you should feel at home there."

"If I am Aphrodite," Aldrina said teasingly, "I should have doves, not waves, in my hands."

"They will come later," Juro said enigmatically.

They sailed on in silence.

Then they started to talk of the things which Aldrina wanted to hear.

Juro told her about Greece, with which he was very familiar.

They talked of Olympus, of the "shining cliffs" of Delphi, and of the Oracle.

"I wish the Oracle were still working," Aldrina said a little wistfully.

"Why do you worry about the future?" Juro asked. "For myself, I am completely content with the present."

"So am I," Aldrina agreed, "and for the moment I would like to go sailing into the far horizon and never come back."

"That is what we will try to do," Juro said quietly.

There was a deep sincerity in his voice that puzzled her.

When they had been sailing for some time, Juro produced a basket of fruit that he had brought aboard with him.

There were grapes and peaches which must have come from hot-houses.

There were also wild figs that had ripened in the sunshine.

They looked delicious, and Juro said:

"This is the ambrosia of the gods. I should have remembered to bring some nectar to go with it, but I will do so another time."

Aldrina looked at him questioningly, and he said almost fiercely:

"You know there will be another time, and many more times — there has to be!"

"That . . . may be a . . . little difficult," Aldrina answered.

She was thinking that when she went back to the Palace she would never see him again.

"Nothing is too difficult if one is determined to get what one wants," Juro said.

Aldrina laughed.

"That is a very philosophical thing to say, but it does not always happen in real life."

She thought, as she spoke, of how she had hoped that the King, even though he was elderly, would look like an older Juro.

But he had been a disappointment.

"You are looking worried," Juro said unexpectedly. "I told you to forget the past and live in the present. We are here, we are alive, and we have found each other.

What more can we ask?"

"Nothing," Aldrina agreed, "except that now, as you know, we have to turn back."

"Not yet," Juro replied.

Aldrina turned round and saw that they were a long way out to sea and the coast-line was only a faint mark on the horizon.

In another quarter of an hour Juro changed course and they headed back.

When they were nearer to the coast, Aldrina saw that inland there were a number of tents painted in brilliant colours.

Beside them were what she realised were Gypsy caravans.

"Why are all those Gypsies congregated there?" she asked.

Juro looked to where she was pointing and said:

"Oh, we are now off the coast of Xanthe and it is a Gypsy Festival. I had forgotten about it. It happens once a year."

"A Festival — for what?" Aldrina enquired.

"The Gypsies in this part of the world meet together and celebrate some special day of importance which they all observe."

He paused and then continued:

"I cannot remember exactly what it is, but I know there is a great deal of merrymaking, dancing, and, of course, Gypsy music, which is very romantic."

Aldrina gave a little cry.

"I have heard about it," she said, "and I remember my father telling me about the Gypsy dancing and how beautiful it is. He too spoke of their music."

"Their music is very romantic, very wild, the most exciting music in the world," Juro said.

"How I would love to hear it!" Aldrina murmured.

She was wondering as she spoke if the Gypsies ever came to Saria.

If they did, would she be allowed to visit the Festival, see the dancing, and listen to them playing?

She could recall now how her Father had said:

"The Gypsy violins excite emotions in those who listen which no other musician can, however skilful he may be."

As they neared the coast, Aldrina could see that there were a great number of tents.

The caravans, which were painted in every conceivable colour, looked striking even from a distance.

"When does the Festival begin?" she asked after a little while when Juro said no more.

"To-morrow night, I believe," he answered. "Then all the musicians gather together and there is dancing when they leap over the fires. Also, of course, there are numerous Fortune-Tellers who can tell what is going to happen to you in the future."

"I long to hear their music," Aldrina said.

She felt as if the Gypsies in their colourful tents and caravans were calling to her.

She felt they had a message that she must hear.

She was sure that if she listened to the violins, she would know what it was.

Impulsively, without thinking, she said:

"Oh, please, please, take me to the Festival! It is something I have never been to, and I may never have a chance like this again."

Juro looked surprised. Then he said:

"You would really like to go?"

"More than I have ever wanted anything in my life!" Aldrina cried. "I want to hear them play and watch them dance."

There was silence for a moment. Then Juro said:

"I suppose it is possible, but you do realise we should have to go dressed as Gypsies, otherwise they will know we are intruders who are there out of curiosity."

Aldrina gave a sigh.

"Then that makes it impossible for me to go, because I have no Gypsy clothes."

Juro's eyes twinkled.

"I think you are offering me a challenge," he said.

Aldrina looked at him.

"You mean . . . oh, please . . . do you really mean that you might . . . take me?"

"I think it might be amusing," he said, "if we went for just a little while. I believe that at the beginning of the Festival everyone behaves themselves. It is only later that they get noisy and sometimes rough."

"We need not stay very long," Aldrina said. "If I could just hear the Gypsy violins, and perhaps see the Gypsies as they leap over the fires, it will be something I shall remember all my life."

"I am sure you will have other things to remember apart from that," Juro said enigmatically. "But, as I said, it is a challenge."

"You mean . . . it is one you . . . will accept?"

"I find it difficult to refuse anything you ask of me," he said quietly.

"Then, please . . . please . . . take me to the Festival! I will come away the minute you tell me to, but I do want to see it! And, as I have already said, it will be something for me always . . . to remember."

She thought as she spoke of how, when she got back to the Palace, there would be no Juro, only the Prime Minister to lecture her, and the Statesmen with their voices droning on as they talked and talked without anything ever seeming to happen.

"I will not listen to them," Aldrina told herself. "Instead, I will hear the Gypsy violins playing."

She looked across the boat at Juro.

"You will take me?" she asked.

"I will take you because you want to go," he said, "but we must be very carefully disguised, since the Gypsies resent being spied upon. They are a very secretive people."

"I have always heard that," Aldrina said. "I have read a lot of books about them and their strange customs, and how terribly persecuted they have been in many countries."

"They are welcome around here," Juro said, "and that is why they usually hold their meetings in the Southern Balkan States, and, of course, in Greece."

Aldrina thought she would have liked to see them in the country which meant so much to her, and which was a part of her blood.

Then she told herself that she would be very content if she could just hear them in Xanthe, and she would have that to remember.

"I will tell you what I will do," Juro said as if he had been thinking it out. "If you will come to me to-morrow evening, when everybody in your house is asleep, I will have a Gypsy dress for you to wear in disguise, and I will take you for a short time to the Festival."

Aldrina gave a little cry but did not interrupt.

"If we ride there when it is dark," Juro went on, "everyone will be too occupied with the dancing and the music to be looking for strangers. Anyway, we will look like Gypsies."

Aldrina clasped her hands together.

"It is the most . . . exciting thing that has ever . . . happened to me," she said, "and . . . thank you . . . thank you!"

"I only hope you will not be disappointed," Juro answered.

They passed the mouth of the River Leeka, and arrived back on Aldrina's beach.

"I will be here to-morrow evening," Aldrina said, "and you are . . . quite certain you do not . . . mind taking . . . me to the Festival?"

Juro smiled.

"It will be an adventure for me too," he said. "After all, the gods and goddesses often disguised themselves so that they could meet ordinary human beings without their being suspicious."

Aldrina laughed as he helped her out of the boat and into the shallow water.

"Take care of yourself," he said.

"I will," she answered, "for if anything happened to me, I could not . . . bear to miss tomorrow evening."

She ran through the water and onto the beach and heard Juro laugh as she did so.

She turned round, but he was already sailing away.

She had a feeling of fear that when he had gone she might never see him again.

When Aldrina arrived back at the Villa, Sophie was up and dressed.

"Where have you been, Drina?" she asked. "I could not find you anywhere."

"I felt I needed some exercise, so I walked along the coast for quite a long way."

She felt her conscience prick her even though it was partly true.

Then she deliberately put the thought away from her mind.

All she wanted to think about now was to-morrow night and how wildly exciting it would be to see him and the Gypsies.

Aldrina ate a very late breakfast, then she and Sophie bathed until it was time for luncheon.

After that she lay on the verandah and fell asleep.

When she awoke she was aware that Sophie was talking to Count Nicolas in a low voice at the other end of the verandah.

"What is it?" she asked. "What has happened?"

"Nothing to upset you," Sophie said quickly, "but Count Nicolas has some news from the Palace."

"What has happened?" Aldrina asked.

She sat up in her chair and said to Count Nicolas, who was standing:

"Sit down and tell me what has occurred."

"Nothing very terrible, Ma'am," he replied with a smile, "except that Prince Inigo is apparently making trouble because Doctor Ansay will not tell him where you are."

"Oh, I hope he does not find out!" Aldrina cried.

"Prince Inigo has found that nobody will answer his questions, and he is in an exceedingly bad temper."

"How dare he behave in such a way!" Aldrina complained. "He has no authority over me, and I think he is a horrible man!"

"So do I," Sophie agreed. "He has always behaved badly. My husband detested him and often told me what trouble he has caused in the City, and about the scandals in which he has been involved."

"I do not want to hear about them," Aldrina said. "I just want to forget him and everything else at the Palace while I am here."

"That is what I hope you will be able to do, Ma'am," the Count said.

"You quite understand," Aldrina said, "that if by any chance the Prince should discover where I am and arrives here, you are not to let him in? I absolutely refuse to see him!"

"I will do my best, Ma'am," the Count promised.

He saluted respectfully, but before he left, Aldrina was aware that he smiled at Sophie.

"I find the Count an extremely charming man," she said.

"Oh, so do I!" Sophie said. "And he is ready to do anything to please us."

"The only thing I want him to do is to keep Prince Inigo away from me," Aldrina said. "I hate him and he frightens me."

"I am not surprised," Sophie agreed. "I too think he is frightening, and he is always so determined to get his own way."

Aldrina felt herself shiver.

She knew exactly what the Prince wanted, and she thought she would rather die than have to marry him.

There was something about him she knew to be evil.

She felt now as if he were thinking of her and somehow pulling her almost by magic towards him.

Then she told herself she was being hysterical.

At the same time, she was afraid.

Only by forcing herself to think of Juro, and only of Juro, could she prevent herself from shivering.

The day passed slowly, and the two women went early to bed.

It was then that Aldrina began to think again of Juro, and regret that she was not meeting him early in the morning.

But she knew that the time it would take him to find their Gypsy disguises would prevent him from taking her sailing with him.

"I want to be with him," she told herself, then she was afraid of her own thoughts.

She had to be sensible.

She had to realise that this was just a chance encounter made on a holiday, and that when she went back to the City she could never see Juro again.

"He is kind, he is trustworthy, and I can talk to him as I have never talked to any other man," she told herself. "But because I am a Queen, I have to be careful not to become too involved."

She thought what a terrible shock it would be to her Ladies-in-Waiting if they knew how she had been behaving.

She wondered what her Prime Minister would say if he knew she had been spending hours with a strange young man about whom she knew nothing.

What was more, he had treated her not as a Monarch, but as if she were an ordinary young girl.

Aldrina told herself she would always remember his compliments.

And she knew it would be difficult ever to forget the way he had looked at her.

She knew without his saying so that he admired her.

It was very exciting to know that the most handsome man she had ever seen thought she was pretty.

Perhaps, although he had not said so, in his eyes she was beautiful — as beautiful as Aphrodite.

Aldrina found it impossible to sleep and turned over and over against her pillows.

She was remembering how Juro had made her blush.

She recalled the silences between them when they were somehow talking to each other without words.

Because it was so easy to talk to him, she was never quite certain whether they were speaking Greek or English.

His English was almost perfect, and she only hoped that her Greek was as good.

It was a long time since she had been able to talk to her Father.

She was half-afraid that sometimes she had forgotten the right word, or pronounced it incorrectly.

Juro! Juro!

The night seemed to be full of him.

She looked up at the stars, feeling he was somehow there among them.

She knew she could always turn to the stars for guidance and help.

She had the feeling that was what she must do now.

She knew in her heart that what she was asking was wrong.

Soon the day must come when she would plead with the stars to help her to forget Juro because she must never see him again.

Slowly the night passed.

Then, at last, there was a flicker in the sky, and the dawn broke.

Aldrina had an impulse to get out of bed and go to their meeting-place, just in case Juro had changed his mind and was there waiting for her.

Then she told herself that if she did so, she would only be disappointed.

Moreover, if Juro got to know of it, he would think she was running after him.

That was something, she told herself, seeing how handsome he was, that many women must have done in the past.

At the idea of it she felt as if a dagger pierced her breast.

It was a pain that came from the very depths of her heart.

chapter five

Aldrina and Sophie swam in the morning, then, after luncheon, lay on the balcony, looking out to sea.

It was then that Sophie began to talk again about her life and of how unhappy she had been.

Aldrina was sure it was good for her to be open about it rather than bottle it up.

She encouraged her to describe how cruel her husband had been and how miserable she had felt day after day.

"I suppose if I had been able to give my husband children," Sophie said at last, "things might have been different. But it was not my fault."

Aldrina did not say anything because she was not quite certain how two people had a child.

She had not thought to ask her mother before she left England.

Not having a Father, she had almost forgotten that a man desired a family and it meant a great deal to him.

She knew, however, that she could never have loved the old King enough to want his children.

"I have been lucky, very lucky," she told herself secretly, "that he should have . . . died."

She knew it was wicked to think such a thing.

At the same time, she knew she had always envisaged that her husband and her children would be handsome.

It was inevitable that she should think of Juro, then she quickly shied away from the idea.

The one thing that was firm in her mind was that he must never know who she really was.

She was quite certain that if he did, he would not wish to be involved with the Queen of Saria and would leave her immediately.

It was then she began to think about her future and realise that it would be very difficult for her ever to take a husband, unless, of course, it was somebody like Prince Inigo, who wanted to rule the country.

No ordinary man would ever aspire to marrying a Queen and would, in fact, be horrified at the idea.

She began to think of the years stretching ahead when the only men she would talk to would be the Prime Minister and the Statesmen.

Because it frightened her, she jumped to her feet.

"Let us go for a walk," she suggested to Sophie.

Sophie shook her head.

"It is too hot, and to be honest, Drina, I am still tired."

Aldrina looked at her and realised there were dark lines under her eyes and she looked pale.

"It *is* hot out here," she agreed. "Let us go inside and I will play the piano to you. I have not touched it since we arrived, and I will play some of my favourite tunes."

She went into the beautiful Sitting-Room, where in a corner stood a piano which, to her surprise, was well tuned.

She sat down, first running her fingers over the keys, before she played some of the melodies her mother had taught her when she was a child.

As she played, she forgot Sophie and began to think of how exciting it would be to hear the Gypsy music.

She thought of the violins as they portrayed all the emotions that were in her heart.

'I suppose I ought to tell Sophie what I am going to do,' she thought.

Then she knew it would be a mistake.

She would have to make so many explanations, and it was obvious that Sophie would ask her about Juro.

She had no wish for the moment to talk about him.

'Perhaps after to-night I shall never see him again,' she thought dully.

She felt a pain come into her breast that she could not ignore.

"I am being stupid, very stupid!" she chided herself, "I am a Queen, and Queens cannot behave as other women can."

She wondered what the Prime Minister and her Ladies-in-Waiting would say if she invited Juro to the Palace.

She was sure they would be horrified.

Then she thought that if she invited him and he refused, that would definitely be the end of the association.

'I want to talk to him, I want to see him, and I want to be with him,' Aldrina cried in her heart.

She knew there was only one answer to that — impossible!

They had finished tea and were sitting talking when the door opened unexpectedly and Count Nicolas came in.

"Excuse me, Your Majesty," he said to Aldrina, "but I have to tell you that Prince

Inigo is here. Although I have tried to prevent him from seeing you, there is nothing more I can do without using physical violence."

Aldrina made a sound of exasperation.

"How can he have found out where we are?" she demanded. "Doctor Ansay was so certain that no one would disturb us."

"I am afraid it is possible, Ma'am, that the Prince has spies in the Palace and, if the bribe is high enough, few people will refuse it."

"Then send him away!" Aldrina said angrily. "I will not see him!"

Even as she spoke the door was pushed open behind the Count and Prince Inigo came into the room.

"So this is where you have vanished to!" he said to Aldrina. "I cannot think why I could not be told where you had gone."

"Your Royal Highness was not informed for the simple reason that I wished to be alone with the Baroness and rest on the Doctor's orders," Aldrina said coldly.

"Then, of course, I am only too willing to rest with you," the Prince said. "I have brought you flowers and some chocolates which I am sure is something you cannot buy in this part of the country."

"That was very kind of you," Aldrina

115

said politely, "but, quite frankly, all I want is to be alone and to sleep as much as possible. So I am afraid your visit is quite unnecessary."

The Prince laughed, and it was not a very pleasant sound.

"You are trying to get rid of me," he said, "but when I have come such along way, you cannot be so heartless as not to allow my horses to rest."

Aldrina drew in her breath.

"What do you mean?"

The Prince smiled at her.

"I mean, of course, that you can at least offer me a bed for the night and accommodate my horses in the stables."

"I am afraid that is impossible," Aldrina said quickly. "The Baroness and I are alone and unchaperoned."

The Prince raised his eye-brows.

"I imagined when I learned who was with you that the Baroness was your chaperon."

There was nothing Aldrina could say to that.

She looked appealingly at the Count.

However, she realised that he was right in saying that he could keep the Prince away only by using force.

Prince Inigo clearly had no intention of leaving.

As if he were aware that he had won the battle, he said:

"What I would like now is a drink, and am sure your very fierce and aggressive Count can order one for me."

He gave the Count an unpleasant look as he spoke.

Aldrina knew that he was annoyed that he had been held up when he arrived.

For the moment she felt helpless and could only say to Count Nicolas:

"Would you be kind enough to ask the servants to bring some wine?"

"Of course, Ma'am," the Count said. "I think there is some champagne in the cellar. Do you wish to join His Royal Highness?"

"Very well," Aldrina said sharply, "but I think it is a mistake for His Royal Highness to stay here this evening."

"Where else can I go?" the Prince asked. "There is not another house within miles of this one, and as I have already said, it would be sheer cruelty to have to take my horses back to the City until they have had at least twenty-four hours' rest."

"I think twelve should be adequate," Aldrina retorted.

She thought, as she spoke, she must somehow make Prince Inigo leave immediately, even if she had to send for Doctor Ansay.

It was then that she realised he was looking at her in a way that she not only disliked but found frightening.

Her perception told her he was thinking that after to-night she would want him to stay.

She did not know why that idea came into her mind, but it was there, and she felt she could read his thoughts.

It was something she had often done with other people.

She began to feel very frightened.

She was sure the Prince was going to find some way of forcing her to accept him as her husband.

At least in the Palace she had been protected by dozens of people in the household.

Here there were only Sophie and Count Nicolas.

She had the uncomfortable conviction that the Prince was plotting to force her to marry him whether she wanted to do so or not.

It flashed through her mind that if she told Count Nicolas to throw him out bodily, he would have to obey her.

But she knew that to do so would ruin

the Count, for somehow the Prince would avenge himself on him.

"What can I do? What can I do?" she asked herself.

Then, as Count Nicolas came into the room to say that a man-servant was bringing in the champagne, she knew the answer.

To-night she would be with Juro.

If the Prince should dare, though it seemed incredible, to break into her bed-room to force his attentions upon her, she would not be there.

The thought was like the sunshine coming in through the window.

The sun itself was sinking into the sea in a blaze of crimson glory.

Soon the first stars would be twinkling above them in the sky, and she knew there would be a full moon.

Juro had told her that the Gypsy Festival always took place when the moon was full.

It would be Juro who would save her, Juro who would make sure that she enjoyed herself with him, untroubled and unafraid.

If the Prince was curious to-morrow as to where she had been, what did it matter?

She would tell him that she had slept on the sand or in the garden.

Anyway, he would surely be too ashamed to admit that he had tried to enter her room.

How otherwise could he know she was not there?

She felt light-hearted that her problem was solved.

When the servant came in with the champagne, she sipped a little of it.

Count Nicolas left them and Prince Inigo, sprawling back in an arm-chair, raised his glass.

"To your beautiful eyes, Aldrina," he said, "and to the future!"

Aldrina deliberately put down the glass she was holding in her hand.

"Sophie and I are not concerned with the future at the moment," she said. "We are forgetting the past and living in the present."

"That is what I too am doing," Prince Inigo said.

The way he spoke and the expression in his eyes made Aldrina shiver.

He was looking pleased with himself because he had achieved his intention to spend the night in the Villa.

She knew this was only the beginning of what he was plotting in his mind.

Abruptly Aldrina rose to her feet.

"I am going to rest before dinner," she said, "and I shall order it early because Sophie and I are, on Doctor's orders, to sleep as much as we possibly can."

Prince Inigo did not answer.

He only looked at her from under his half-closed eyes.

He reminded her of a serpent as it swayed to and fro, moving closer and closer towards its victim.

It was with difficulty that she left the room without running and went upstairs.

She rang for Lucy, and the English maid came at once to undo her gown.

"I 'ears as you've got company for dinner, Yer Majesty," she remarked.

"Not on my invitation," Aldrina replied. "I wanted to be very quiet while I was here, and I cannot imagine how His Highness discovered where I was staying."

"I 'pects everybody knows at the Palace," Lucy said. "Although I don't understand what they're sayin', it's chatter, chatter, chatter all day long, and they hates 'Is Royal 'Ighness — I can see that!"

Aldrina wanted to say that she hated him too, but knew it would be wrong to do so.

"Well, all I hope is that he leaves tomorrow," she said aloud.

She then busied herself choosing a gown

from those that were hanging in the wardrobe.

She was thinking that Juro had never seen her except in a bathing-dress.

She wondered if he would think she looked elegant in an evening-gown.

Finally she chose a simple one of white muslin.

She had, of course, not brought with her to the Villa the elaborate Court gowns that were in her trousseau.

Fortunately, because she was a bride, she had also some simple white gowns.

The black ones she had bought after the King's death were of a thicker material and too hot to wear in this weather.

The white muslin gown was very light, and she thought becoming.

She hoped that Juro would admire her in it.

She wondered what was his taste in women.

Because he was Greek, did he like the black-haired Greek women with their flashing dark eyes?

She looked at her reflection in the mirror and saw that the sun had accentuated the touches of red in her fair curls.

Luckily her skin never burnt with the sun.

Her mother had once said it was because of her Greek blood.

She looked at herself for a long time, until she remembered that Lucy was waiting for her to lie down on the bed.

"Try to sleep, Ma'am," she said, "an' I'll bring in your bath at seven o'clock."

She left the room, and Aldrina watched through the window as the last streak of crimson sank into the sea.

Now she could see the first evening star shining faintly in the sky.

She looked at it and said:

"You have to help me . . . you must help me to get rid of Prince Inigo, and please . . . please let Juro . . . stay with . . . me and not . . . find out who . . . I am."

She thought, as she spoke, that the stars had already helped her.

They had stopped him from coming to the Villa when she had first invited him.

If he had done so, it would have been so easy for him to find out by an inadvertent word, or perhaps a bow, that she was not an ordinary young woman, but a Queen and a widow.

"He must never know . . . he must never know," she repeated to the stars.

She thought that if she were very lucky she could continue to see him for at least as long as she stayed at the Villa.

He thought she belonged to the sea, and not to reality.

Dinner was an uncomfortable meal with Prince Inigo boasting about himself.

She knew he was trying to impress them with his importance.

Aldrina found him continually looking at her in a way she most disliked.

It made it difficult for her to concentrate on what she was eating.

She realised that he had ordered another bottle of champagne and consumed most of it himself.

As they went into the Dining-Room he had said:

"As I am not dining with one, but with two beautiful ladies, I will sit between them."

As he spoke he had seated himself at the head of the table.

It was the seat that Aldrina had naturally sat in ever since she had come to the Villa.

The Prince then gave orders to the servants.

He talked to Aldrina, ignoring the Baroness as if she were of no consequence.

He appeared to be quite unabashed that the "beautiful ladies," as he called them, had nothing whatever to say to him.

In fact, they did not have a chance to speak because he talked and talked until the meal was finished.

It was then that Aldrina rose from the table and walked towards the door.

The Prince was on the point of following her, but stopped to order the man-servant to bring him some brandy.

As she reached the Sitting-Room, Aldrina realised this was her opportunity.

"Tell His Royal Highness I have gone to bed," she said to Sophie.

She then ran out through the French windows, across the garden, and down the twisting path which led to the beach.

She would be out of sight of the Sitting-Room, she thought, before the Prince could come from the Dining-Room.

Once she was on the beach she knew she would be safe.

She would be too early for Juro, but at least no one could stop her now from leaving the Villa.

The Prince would not be able to follow her, since he must accept her message that she had gone to bed.

'I am free!' she thought with a leap of her heart.

Because it was difficult to walk in high-heeled shoes, she took them off and walked in her stocking feet.

The sand felt warm, having been baked by the sun all day.

Now the air was cooler and there was just the music of the very small waves as they rippled softly on one side of her.

She walked on, wondering how long she would have to wait for Juro.

Then her heart leapt as she saw at their meeting-place there was a boat.

She had not noticed it sooner because it had no sail.

Then, as she hurried eagerly towards it, she was aware that there were two men with the boat besides Juro.

He was standing looking in her direction, as if he knew instinctively that she would come earlier than they had planned.

It was with difficulty that Aldrina, because she was so excited, did not run the last few yards and throw herself against him.

Instead, she forced herself to move slowly.

But her eyes were on him and she thought he was even more handsome than she remembered.

As she reached him he said quietly:

"You have come! I was half-afraid you might have changed your mind."

"How could I do anything so stupid?" Aldrina asked. "You know I am longing to see the Gypsies' Festival."

His eyes twinkled as if he expected she might have said something different.

Then he said:

"I only hope you will not be disappointed, and I have brought a costume which I hope will please you."

Aldrina wanted to say that anything would please her if he would take her to the Festival.

But she thought it might sound pushing, and instead she just smiled at him.

As if it were an after-thought, she looked at the boat.

The two seamen pulled it up on the sand and Juro helped Aldrina into it without her stepping into the water.

When he climbed in beside her, the two seamen pushed the boat out and started to row.

It was then that Aldrina became aware for the first time that there was a yacht standing some way out to sea.

She had not noticed it as she came from the Villa.

She realised they were rowing towards it, and she asked:

"Is that your yacht?"

"I thought it would be a good place to change," Juro explained. "As you know, we have to be very well disguised, otherwise the Gypsies will be suspicious that we are there to spy on them."

He was speaking in English so that the two seamen would not understand what he said.

Aldrina was silent until they reached the yacht.

They climbed aboard, and although it was not very large, she felt that it was an extremely attractive vessel.

It was beautifully decorated with everything shining as if its crew took great pains to keep it ship-shape.

They passed the Saloon, and Juro took her down the companionway.

He showed her into a cabin which she thought was very attractive.

It had white walls and a carpet and curtains in soft pink.

It was obviously a cabin designed for a woman.

Aldrina could not help wondering how many beautiful women Juro had brought aboard before, and who had slept there.

She then saw the clothes lying on the bed.

As she looked at them she realised that Juro really had supplied her with a complete Gypsy outfit.

"I suggest you change, but may I tell you

that you look very lovely in that white gown and exactly how I thought you would look."

Aldrina smiled at him.

"It seems incredible that I have always been in a bathing-dress until now."

"I told you that you came from the sea," he answered.

His eyes met hers, and for a moment it was difficult to look away.

Then he said abruptly:

"Hurry and change. We have some way to go."

He went from the cabin and shut the door.

Aldrina started to undress.

As she put on the Gypsy clothes she found they were exactly what she wanted — a full red skirt over two starched white petticoats and an embroidered blouse that had small sleeves.

Then there was a black velvet bodice which laced down the front.

It was the sort of costume which the Gypsies had worn for centuries, and there was little variation from country to country.

When she was dressed, finding to her surprise that the clothes fitted her exactly, she wondered what she should do about her hair.

Gypsies were traditionally dark, whether they came from the Balkan countries, France, Spain, or anywhere else.

There was a large red handkerchief on the bed, and she was contemplating how she should wear it when there was a knock on the door.

"May I come in?" Juro asked.

"Yes, please do," she replied.

He came in and she saw that he was wearing clothes that she was sure were usually worn by the more important men of the Gypsy tribe.

They certainly became him.

Round his head he had a red scarf that always made Gypsy men look handsome and romantic.

When he looked at her, Juro knew without words what was worrying her.

"If you are thinking about your hair, I am going to plait it for you, and then you must hide it under a veil I have brought so that you do not attract attention."

She nodded and he added:

"I shall be jealous if you do, and it would also be dangerous."

"That is what I was thinking," Aldrina agreed.

He made her sit down in front of the dressing-table which was built into the wall.

Standing behind her, he plaited her hair so skilfully that inevitably she wondered how many women's hair he had plaited previously.

When he reached the end of her hair, which reached nearly to her waist, he wound the plait round her head.

He pinned it with hair-pins which were lying in a box on the dressing-table.

"You think of everything!" she said admiringly.

"I try to," he answered. "This is your adventure, and if we undertake one, we must do it properly or not at all."

When her hair was in place he put over it first the red handkerchief which had lain on the bed.

Then he covered it with a beautiful veil fringed with coins.

It hung down her back and sparkled with every move she made.

There were also coins along her forehead, and she thought as she looked in the mirror that they were very becoming.

Juro went away to fetch some bracelets from which also dangled coins and charms.

They were not valuable, but Aldrina knew they were what the Gypsies would wear and therefore a necessary part of her costume.

When Juro had finished, she thought no lady's-maid could have been more skilful or made her look more attractive.

"Thank you . . . thank you . . . very much!" she said delightedly.

She had already found the shoes he had put by the bed to go with the outfit, and they were black which matched her stockings.

To her surprise, they also fitted and were, in fact, very comfortable.

In keeping with the way Juro had thought of every detail, she realised they were not expensive, but shoes a Gypsy could afford to buy from an ordinary shoe-shop.

As she took one last look at her reflection in the mirror, she thought she no longer looked like herself.

She was sure that no one would for a moment be suspicious that she was anything but a true Romany.

Then Juro sat down in the chair she had just vacated and drew something from his pocket.

It was a black eye-shade, and he put it over one of his eyes.

"Why are you doing that?" she asked in surprise.

"We are well disguised," he explained,

"but there is just a chance that in this part of the world someone might recognise me and know I was not a Gypsy and had no right to be at the Festival."

"Yes, of course," Aldrina said, "and I think it was very clever of you to have thought of it."

He certainly looked strange with his left eye covered.

At the same time, it gave him a raffish appearance, and made Aldrina think that he looked more like a pirate than a Gypsy.

Juro rose from the chair and held out his hand.

"Now," he said, "our adventure begins, and you will feel as romantic as you want to when you hear the violins."

They walked up on deck.

By now the last of the sun had disappeared and the stars were coming out in the sky.

The moon was rising, casting its silver light on the water.

As she looked up at it, Aldrina was aware that she could hear in the distance the sound of music.

It was very faint, but it was there.

She thought excitedly that it was calling her: calling her to the Gypsy Festival.

They climbed down from the deck and into the rowing-boat.

It was clear that Juro had already given instructions to the two men, who started to pull away from the yacht and move swiftly towards the mouth of the river.

There was quite some distance to go until they entered it.

The river was still quite wide even after they had passed through the mouth.

Aldrina thought it a good thing to have what was almost a Channel between Saria and Prince Terome.

It reminded her of the English Channel which on a much larger scale divided England from France.

Now she could see the spires and towers of Xanthe, and the music she had heard faintly in the distance grew louder until it was almost overpowering.

It was then she realised that there was not just one Band playing, but a number of them all playing together.

Then mingled with the sound of the violins was the heavy beat of drums and the hoot of trumpets.

They reached a wooden quay.

It was in darkness and completely quiet, and there was not even a light to be seen in any of the houses.

Then, as if he knew what she was wondering, Juro said:

"They start the celebrations with a march of the Xanthe Bands and make a noise which, I assure you, has nothing to do with the Gypsies."

Aldrina laughed.

"It is certainly not very romantic," she said.

The men rowed until they came to a small landing-point on the quay.

The two oarsmen pulled the boat alongside.

Juro got out and helped Aldrina up beside him.

He talked in a language she did not understand before he took her by the hand.

They walked along the wooden quay towards the lights and noise of the Bands which were gradually retreating into the distance.

chapter six

As Aldrina's eyes became accustomed to the darkness, she realised that beyond the quay there was an enormous building.

As if she asked the question, Juro said:

"That is the Palace. It was originally a fortress and stands right on the bank of the river which divides Xanthe from her enemies."

"You mean," Aldrina said, "that Xanthe was fighting Saria?"

"That is right," Juro replied. "Saria and Ravalla, and for that matter a number of other countries also. They were very aggressive."

"Then I hope there will be no more wars," Aldrina murmured.

She was speaking to herself rather than to him.

She thought how disastrous it would be if she were in charge of a country at war.

Obviously she had no idea of how to fight an enemy.

The road along which they were walking came to an end.

The drums and trumpets had stopped

and the music Aldrina now heard was, she knew, Gypsy music.

In a few seconds more they came into the open and she saw, as she expected, the brilliant colours of the Gypsies.

They were grouped in a large open space in front of the Palace.

That part of it which backed onto the river might have looked like a fortification, but on the other side the frontage was ablaze with light from a multitude of windows.

Marble steps led down in terraces to the open ground on which the Gypsies were assembled.

There were hundreds and hundreds of them, and more kept coming in from where she knew they were camped down by the sea.

The Gypsy women in their red skirts and their veils sparkling with coins similar to those she was wearing were extremely attractive.

She recognised the *Voivodes*, who were wearing silver buttons, and a number were in red coats.

She realised as she looked at them that Juro had made himself a *Voivode* because there were silver buttons on his coat too.

He took her by the arm and steered her

through the crowds of Gypsies.

When they reached the first terrace rising up towards the Palace, just in front of them some people who were obviously onlookers moved away from the stone seat on which they had been watching.

Juro sat down on it and pulled Aldrina down beside him.

Now she was a little higher than the people gathering in front of them, and it was easy to see exactly what was happening.

The music came from a group of musicians at one side, and she guessed that there must be at least twenty violins and even more lutes.

There was, she saw, a fire being lit in the centre of the ground, and as the Gypsies moved into groups, Juro pointed out to her the tribes that he recognised.

There were the *Kalderash*, who were copper-and tin-smiths.

Then he pointed out the *Sastrari*, workers in iron, and the *Anatori*, tin-smiths or -platers who, Juro explained, had recently arrived from Turkey.

Next there were the *Tajari*, the lock- and bolt-smiths, and, of course, the *Laoutari*, the musicians to whom she was now listening.

It was all very exciting.

Then the noise of voices ceased, the Gypsy women assembled round the fire, and Aldrina realised that the dancing was about to begin.

The *Kalderash* women, wearing necklaces and gold coins and huge ear-rings to match, were better dressed than any of the rest.

The violins burst into the wild, joyous sound of the Gypsy dance, and the women began to move hand-in-hand around the fire.

Then each one loosed herself from the ring and began to dance, at first slowly and gracefully, then with movements which quickened and grew wilder and more exaggerated.

They danced for some time, then, as they moved away, the music changed and became more entrancing and tender.

Other Gypsy women took their place and a crowd of women and men began to sing.

It was a beguiling melody, and their voices seemed to blend not only with the music, but also with the stars in the sky above them.

The moonlight was turning the Palace and the people dancing around the fire to silver.

At first the sound of their singing was delicate and it seemed to tinkle like silver bells.

Then it became wild, invigorating, and exciting.

Aldrina felt as if it drew her heart from her body and she became one with it.

Quicker and quicker the melody rose and quicker and quicker the dancers moved.

Every pirouette, every step, seemed to accelerate as the music grew wilder.

Then they began to leap over the fire with a grace which made them look as if they wore invisible wings.

Aldrina felt as if the intensity of what she was hearing was almost too much to bear.

Suddenly the wild throbbing ceased and the music was replaced with a soft, sweet melody which seemed like the coming of a rainbow after a storm.

It was then, as Aldrina drew in her breath, that she realised she was holding on tightly to Juro's hand.

She saw too that Juro was not looking at the Gypsies dancing, but at her.

She took a deep breath and felt as if she had not breathed for a long time.

Then, with a little shudder because she

had felt so intense, she took her hand away from Juro's.

"I thought you would feel like that," he said in a deep voice.

"It was wonderful! Wonderful!" she cried.

When the music stopped, the dancers stood for a moment with their arms stretched up towards the sky.

There had been silence from all those watching.

Now the voices all round rose again, and as Aldrina tried to come back to reality she realised that a little way from them was a noisy group of men and women talking and laughing and sounding as if they had had too much to drink.

She glanced towards them, and as she did so she saw that two men in elaborate livery had approached and stopped beside them.

They spoke to Juro in a language she did not understand, and she wondered what they were saying to him.

It seemed as if he were trying to refuse to do something they wanted.

Then, as they spoke again, he said to her:

"We have been sent for by His Royal Highness Prince Terome, and I am afraid we have to obey his command."

Aldrina was frightened.

She remembered what she had heard about the Prince.

As Juro rose to his feet to obey, he realised that the Prince was one of the noisy party on the terrace above them.

The liveried servants were on each side of them, and there was nothing they could do but walk to where she could see now there were over twenty people in the group.

They were clustered around a man who was sitting on an elaborate chair almost like a throne.

Because she was nervous, Aldrina slipped her hand again into Juro's.

As his fingers closed over hers, she felt comforted by the strength of them.

"He will protect me," she told herself.

At the same time, she was not at all certain what he was to protect her from.

It took them a few seconds to reach the Prince where he was sitting with two over-painted and over-bejewelled women beside him.

The men with him were making a great deal of noise.

One look at them told Aldrina she had been right in thinking they had had too much to drink.

The Prince himself was sprawling in his chair in an abandoned manner.

As she looked at him, Aldrina was sure that the stories she had heard about him were not exaggerated.

He certainly appeared very debauched: There were bags under his eyes, and she thought, as their eyes met, that he was undoubtedly evil.

Because she remembered she must behave as a Gypsy, she curtsied very low, and Juro bowed to the Prince as they stood in front of him.

As she rose from her curtsy the Prince said to Juro:

"That is a very pretty Gypsy woman you have there. How much do you want for her?"

He was speaking in Greek, and Aldrina understood what he said.

At the same time, she could hardly believe that she had not misinterpreted his words.

Juro bowed his head again.

"I am flattered by Your Royal Highness's compliments," he said, speaking in the same language, "but the woman is not for sale."

"Nonsense!" the Prince said sharply. "Everyone has his price, and I will pay you handsomely for anything so exquisite."

There was a roar of laughter as Prince Terome said this, and one or two of the others said in slurred voices:

"Make him pay! He can afford it! Make him pay for what he wants."

Aldrina's hand tightened on Juro's, and he said in the polite manner of speaking he had used before:

"There is no money in the world that would buy this woman from me."

"Do not prevaricate," Prince Terome snapped. "I find her very desirable and I wish her to come with me back to the Palace. There are plenty of other women here for you to choose from."

The irritation was now plain to see on his face.

This made Aldrina wonder whether she should try to run away.

But there were servants on the terrace below them, and she was sure that to please the Prince they would catch her and bring her back.

She made a move a little nearer to Juro, and after a moment he said:

"Perhaps I should explain, Your Royal Highness, that I am betrothed to the woman with me. We have already taken steps of going before the *Voivode* who has blessed us and consented to our marriage, which will take place to-morrow or the day after."

Prince Terome would have spoken angrily, but as he bent forward to do so, Juro went on:

"If any other man should touch her now that she belongs to me, I will curse him with every curse that exists, and so will every member of my tribe. And, if I told them what had happened, so would every Gypsy who is here on Your Royal Highness's grounds."

He paused, and then went on very seriously:

"Our curses have been handed down through the centuries and are very strong, so strong that it is doubtful if Your Royal Highness would live for long after we have cursed you here to-night under the full moon."

Juro's voice rang out as he spoke.

Aldrina was aware that the giggling and joking men and women clustered round the Prince had for the moment fallen silent.

As he finished speaking, Juro bowed, and because he pressed her hand, Aldrina knew she should curtsy, which she did.

Then Juro turned away, intending to

walk down the steps in front of the Prince.

But he had taken hardly a step when the Prince shouted out:

"Wait!"

Juro and Aldrina came to a standstill.

"Wait!" he said again. "I have an idea. If you are to marry, why should we be deprived of the pleasure of attending the marriage this evening, which is certainly something which has not taken place at the Palace for a long time."

"A good idea, Sire, a great idea!" a number of his attendants agreed enthusiastically. "Let us watch them have a Gypsy wedding."

"No, not a Gypsy wedding," the Prince explained. "Instead of their cursing me, I will honour them with a Royal wedding — why not? They shall wed as if they were of Royal blood!"

There was a shriek of laughter at this, and the women cried:

"We can be the Bridesmaids to the Bride, and the men can be the Best Man and the grooms for the Bridegroom."

They all began to exclaim at once, and Prince Terome rose from his chair.

"Follow me!" he ordered Aldrina and Juro.

Frantically Aldrina wondered what would happen if they refused to do so and disappeared into the crowd below.

Even as she thought of it, the servants moved up behind them, and she knew if they attempted to escape they would be caught and brought back.

"What shall we do?" she asked Juro in a whisper, speaking in English.

"There is nothing we can do," he answered, "but try to be brave. It was my fault for bringing you here."

He was speaking in a very low voice, little above a whisper, and Aldrina said:

"You will not let them . . . take me away . . . from you?"

"I think I have already made them realise that is impossible," Juro replied.

They followed the Prince up the steps.

The Prince's Courtiers were talking to him all the time, telling him how they thought a Royal Wedding should be conducted and making a joke of the whole thing.

Some of them stumbled as they walked, and the women were giggling in a silly manner.

There was nothing Juro or Aldrina could do but walk with them into the Palace.

Now the Prince was giving various orders to the servants who were in attendance.

As they hurried to obey his commands,

he went into a room which was luxuriously furnished.

Here he told his friends, still speaking in Greek, what they were to do.

"You will dress in the clothes which I have sent for," he said. "The men will wear Royal Orders and decorations which will be brought from the Tower in which they are kept under guard."

He paused and then continued:

"We will then proceed to the Chapel, where the marriage will take place, and after that, we will 'Bed the Bride.'"

There were more shrieks of laughter at this, and lewd remarks, none of which, fortunately, Aldrina could understand.

She was, however, aware that Juro was furiously angry.

He was standing close beside her, looking, she thought, disdainful and as if he were infinitely superior to the Prince and his associates.

Quicker than she could believe it possible, the servants came back carrying Royal robes consisting of red velvet cloaks trimmed with ermine.

The men and women put them on.

Other servants came from a different direction carrying an unbelievable amount of jewels.

There were crowns, tiaras, ropes of pearls, parures, and huge emerald and ruby necklaces and bracelets, rings and ear-rings.

They sparkled and glittered in the light of the candles and made everything seem so unreal that Aldrina could not help wondering if she was dreaming.

While the men-servants were placing what looked like a Peer's Robe of State on Juro, the maids were encircling Aldrina.

They fixed to her shoulders a long train embroidered with diamanté and edged with ermine.

It looked very strange falling behind her Gypsy dress.

They took off her veil that was glittering with coins.

For one ghastly moment she thought they were going to remove the red silk handkerchief with which Juro had concealed the colour of her hair.

She was panic-stricken in case, if it were seen that she was fair, the Prince might ask a number of uncomfortable questions.

Fortunately the maids drew over her head a veil which reached nearly to the floor in front and trailed down over her train at the back.

They placed a crown set with diamonds

and rubies on her head, and hung round her neck a six-row necklace of pearls which reached nearly to her waist.

Then, as if conjured up by some Fairy Queen rather than Prince Terome, a bouquet of flowers was thrust into her hands.

The Prince, laughing with amusement, then started to lead the way to the Chapel.

He walked ahead.

Giggling and laughing, the women and men followed behind Aldrina and Juro.

Aldrina found her train very heavy, and she was sagging a little until one of the servants, realising her difficulty, picked up the end and carried it.

After that she was able to keep up with Juro.

When they were side by side in a corridor where she thought she would not be overheard, Aldrina said to Juro in a whisper:

"What can we do?"

"Nothing," Juro said abruptly. "The Service will not be legal."

Aldrina, looking at the Prince, thought that no decent man would allow such a mockery to take place in a Church.

She glanced at Juro and realised that he was even angrier than he had been before.

She was, however, aware that they were completely helpless.

She could only hope that the Prince would quickly become bored and look for his amusement elsewhere.

They reached the Chapel, which was at the side of the Palace and, Aldrina thought, very ancient.

There were seven silver lanterns suspended from the ceiling, and the altar itself was ablaze with candle-light.

Standing waiting for them, as he must have been ordered to do, was a Priest wearing white vestments.

The Prince swaggered up in front of him.

"I have brought you two converts to the faith, Father, and make sure you tie the knot properly, so that there is no escape."

The Priest did not answer, but the Prince roared with laughter as he threw himself down in the Bishop's chair in the Chancel.

Aldrina and Juro could do nothing but stand and face the Priest.

"What are your names?" he asked.

Aldrina thought it would be a mistake to reply "Drina" in case the perverted Prince Terome might in some way connect it with the Queen of Saria.

"Mary," she replied, which was in fact the first name by which she had been christened.

Juro answered with "Miklos."

The bouquet was taken away from Aldrina by one of the attendant women who staggered as she walked.

The Service began, and two of the Prince's friends held what Aldrina guessed were the crowns of the Royal House of Xanthe over her and Juro's head.

Aldrina did not let go of Juro's hand, and stood as near to him as she could.

A ring was produced with a huge emerald attached, which was placed on her finger by Juro.

The Service was a short one, and as it took place Aldrina was perceptively aware that the Priest was resenting this farce but was powerless to put a stop to it.

Only as he turned his back on them to kneel down in front of the altar did she realise that the Service was finished.

She could only pray that Juro was right when he said it was not legal.

Now with screams and yells the attendants took over.

"Let us 'Bed the Bride!' " they shouted.

Once again the Prince was leading them in the direction he wished them to go.

Aldrina found herself swept off her feet, not by the women, who she thought would be incapable in their drunken state of carrying her, but by four of the men.

Juro was being carried by a number of other men.

They went up a flight of stairs, and the Prince flung open a door and walked into a room.

It was dominated by a huge bed with a head-board made of mother-of-pearl shells surmounted by a carved and painted crown.

A number of the women, screaming with delight, started to undress Aldrina.

To her relief, she saw that Juro had been carried to another room.

They snatched off her red skirt and exclaimed in surprise at the elegance of her lace-trimmed petticoats and the under-clothes that were beneath them.

She wondered whether, if she screamed, they would stop, but with the noise they were making she knew it would do no good.

When they removed the handkerchief from her head they did not unpin her hair, and Aldrina could only hope they were all too drunk to notice it was fair.

Then, dressed in a frilly nightgown that seemed to have appeared from nowhere, they lifted her onto the bed.

Juro was then brought into the room

wearing a long silk nightshirt.

He was pushed into the bed beside her and then a number of the men disappeared from the room.

They quickly came back carrying in their hands the traditional "Benediction Posset" that was always given to a Bride and Groom if they were "bedded."

Aldrina had read in her books that this happened in France, Spain, Italy, and England, especially in Stuart times, when it was greatly in vogue.

The huge goblet contained, she remembered, milk, wine, honey and eggs, sugar, cinnamon, and nutmeg.

Occasionally, and doubtless on this occasion, there would be cobwebs and soot.

There would also no doubt be a number of other even more unpleasant ingredients which these drunken Courtiers would think amusing.

They handed the goblet first to her, and because she could do nothing else, she drank a tiny sip of it.

It tasted rather better than she expected, and then it was held to Juro's lips.

They tried to force down his throat everything that was in the goblet.

However, he was too strong for them and sent the goblet flying through the air to crash against the wall and spill all of its contents.

This fortunately amused rather than angered their tormentors.

After this, as in England, came the custom of "throwing the stocking."

The Best Man and the groomsmen seated themselves on Juro's side of the bed facing away from the middle of it.

The women did the same on Aldrina's side.

Each "Bride-Knight," as the men were called, and the bridesmaids held a stocking in their hand which was supposed to belong to the Bride and Groom.

On this occasion the stockings had been provided by one of the servants.

The Prince, shouting at the top of his voice, gave the signal.

The stockings were flung backwards over the shoulders of those who held them towards Aldrina and Juro.

If they struck the head of either the Bride or the Bridegroom, it meant that the thrower would soon be married.

Aldrina knew this meant a general outcry of congratulations.

However, the Courtiers were far too drunk to aim anything, let alone a stocking.

They merely fell down over their backs,

or else landed in the centre of the bed.

The Prince then ordered that they were all to attend the "Wedding Feast" and would come back later to ascertain whether or not the marriage had been consummated.

The attendants left amid cries of delight and vulgar advice to the Bride and Bridegroom.

Finally the last guests, who were far more drunk than the others, staggered away.

The next minute Juro jumped from the bed, went to the door, and made sure it was securely shut.

He was aware that the key had been taken from the lock.

He therefore moved a heavy chest-of-drawers in front of it and pulled several chairs on top as Aldrina watched him.

She was thinking despairingly that however much he might try to barricade the door, the Prince would find a way in.

Juro picked up a candelabrum with three candles from the bedside.

He opened the window and stepped through onto what Aldrina thought would be a balcony.

Then he lifted the candelabrum high above his head and made some motions across it with his left hand.

He came back into the room.

"Hurry and get dressed," he said.

Then he disappeared into the room where he had undressed.

He was away for only two or three minutes.

When he returned he was wearing the clothes in which he had come to the Festival, with the exception of his coat.

Aldrina was standing miserably in the other room.

"What is the matter?" he asked.

"M-my clothes . . . have all . . . gone!" she answered. "What . . . on earth shall I . . . do?"

Juro walked to the bed and, pulling off the cover which was of satin and lace, he made of it a shawl.

It crossed over her breasts and he knotted it behind her.

Then he went back to the window, drawing her with him.

As she did so, she realised they were in a room at the back of the Palace and the river lay just below them.

As she looked down, she saw to her joy the yacht which they had left out to sea.

She just had a quick glance before Juro pushed her back.

It was at that moment that something came up through the air and crashed against the stone balcony.

As Juro stepped forward she saw it was a rope tied to an iron hook as used by steeple-jacks.

It was caught onto the stone balustrade of the balcony, and Juro tugged at it to make sure it was secure.

Then he asked:

"Are you strong enough to slide down it?"

Aldrina looked down, and it seemed an enormously long way down to the river below them.

She shivered before she said:

"I . . . I know you will . . . despise me for it . . . but I . . . am . . . afraid."

Juro smiled.

"In which case," he said, "you will have to trust yourself to me."

He went to the side of the window, where there was a curtain cord.

Removing it, he put it round his waist, then round Aldrina's.

It was thick and strong and made of many silken threads.

He tied it into a knot so that she was as close to him as she could possibly be.

Then he said gently:

"Put your arms round my neck, but do

not throttle me! Shut your eyes and pray. I swear that you will be completely safe in my arms."

He held her very close to him as he spoke, and she felt a little thrill go through her which was different from anything she had ever known before.

He was touching her, and her face was hidden in his shoulder while her arms were round his neck.

'I love him,' she thought, 'and if I never see him again, I shall remember this.'

She was hardly aware that he was easing them both over the edge of the balcony.

Then, as they began to slide down the rope, she felt a sudden terror like the stab of a dagger in case they should fall onto something hard which would kill them.

Or perhaps they might even fall into the river, where it was possible they would be drowned.

She held her breath, then from sheer fear she must have become unconscious.

The next thing she knew, Juro was carrying her down the companionway of the yacht and along the corridor.

He took her into the cabin where she had changed earlier that evening before they left for Xanthe.

Very gently he set her down on the bunk,

pulling the sheets and blankets over her.

Then he said in a voice she had never heard him use before:

"Go to sleep, my darling. Everything will be all right when you wake up in the morning."

As he finished speaking, his lips were on hers.

She knew, as he kissed her, and she had never been kissed before, that if she died now, she would already have found paradise.

She belonged to Juro completely and absolutely, as she had always wanted to belong to the man she loved.

Then, as he left her and she heard the cabin door close behind him, the engines accelerated.

With a sigh of relief she knew they were both out of danger.

chapter seven

Aldrina dreamed that Juro was kissing her, and as she opened her eyes she realised he was.

He was kissing her very gently, and because his lips were touching hers, she felt a shaft of sunlight flicking through her body.

She thought how much she loved him.

"Wake up, my darling," he said. "We have something very important to do."

"Wh-what is . . . that?" Aldrina managed to ask.

"We are going to be married," he answered.

She looked up at him.

"M— married?"

"Last night we were in fact legally married," he explained, "but I do not want you to remember that occasion as an important one in your life."

Because Aldrina was speechless, she could only stare at him.

He went on:

"I want you! I want you more than I have ever wanted anyone in my life! I will marry you, and I want you to remember that we started our marriage with happiness and with the blessing of God."

Because she was still bewildered by what he was saying and at the same time moved by the sincerity in his voice, Aldrina could only look up at him.

But no words would come to her lips.

Juro bent a little nearer to her.

"I love you," he said very quietly, "and once we are married I will be able to show you how much you mean to me, and how my heart is your heart."

He kissed her again, then was gone from the cabin before she could ask him any more questions.

Because he had told her what to do, she got out of bed and for a moment could not remember whether or not she had any clothes to put on.

Then with difficulty she recalled that it was here in this cabin that she had changed into her Gypsy clothes before the Festival.

She opened the cupboard which, like the rest of the furniture, was built into the walls and saw her white muslin gown hanging in it.

'At least it is white,' she thought.

At the same time, she almost gave a little cry because it could not really be true that she was going to marry Juro for the second time.

Now there was no doubt it would be legal and she would be his wife.

The whole picture of what she was doing seemed to materialise in front of her eyes.

She could see the horror and consternation on the faces of the Prime Minister and the Statesmen when she returned to the Palace with a husband, a man of whom they had no knowledge whatsoever.

Then, as she thought about the difficulties they would both encounter and how they might in some way hurt Juro, she knew she must abdicate.

She would give up the throne to Prince Inigo, which was exactly what he wanted.

Queen Victoria might be furious with her, and so would the Marquess of Salisbury.

There had been other Statesmen, also, in England who had spoken to her about her duty before she left for Saria.

They had made it clear to her that she was important to the King, and to his country, simply because she was English.

She gave a little sigh.

She wanted to do her best, and she knew her mother would be bitterly disappointed in her if she failed in the task she had undertaken.

But love came first, and the love she had for Juro was so overwhelming.

It was a part of her mind, her heart, and her soul, and it was impossible to think of anything else except that she would be his wife.

If, as he now said, the marriage last night was actually legal, then there would be a scandal if the Prime Minister tried to dissolve it.

How could she possibly explain what had happened?

She had talked to a strange man on the beach, and she had gone with him disguised as a Gypsy to the Festival in Xanthe without letting any of her attendants know what she was doing.

She had become involved with Prince Terome and his disgusting associates.

She could imagine how shocking such behaviour would appear to her subjects in Saria.

There would be those who would laugh and make rude remarks about the fact that she and Juro had been "bedded" in the traditional manner.

Then the Prince and his friends had gone away, intending to return to see if the marriage had been consummated.

The more she thought of what had occurred, the more she knew that abdication was better than letting what had happened last night be known to the Public.

The sun was streaming through the portholes in her cabin, and she looked up at the sky.

She could almost see the stars, and knew she must tell them what she was going to do.

"It is not right," she said a little helplessly, "but there is nothing else I can do."

She put on her white muslin gown.

She was trying to put her hair into some sort of order with the help of pins, when there was a knock on the cabin door.

When she called "Come in," a servant appeared carrying a wreath in his hand.

It was a wreath of white flowers, skilfully made so that it was like a small crown.

The man bowed, then put the wreath down on the dressing-table beside her.

Then, bowing again, he left the cabin without saying a word.

She picked up the wreath and put it on her head.

Instantly she was transformed.

It gave her a grace and a spirituality which was almost like a halo.

It was so marvellous of Juro, she thought, to give her something special to wear at her wedding when she had no veil.

'He thinks of everything, and he loves me,' she told herself.

Then she felt just a little tremor of fear.

Perhaps when he knew who she was he would be shocked at her wishing to abdicate from her responsibilities, even for his sake.

People, all people, especially in this part of the world, looked up to Royalty and expected them to be leaders in their country.

It might sound romantic to say that she was giving up everything for love.

At the same time, there would be a great number of people who would condemn her totally for shrinking from her responsibilities.

"There is nothing else I can do," she said again defensively, as if she were being accused.

She was looking at herself in the mirror.

She did not see the beautiful picture she made, but only the worried expression on her mother's face, and the anger on that of the Prime Minister and the Statesmen — the triumphant expression in Prince Inigo's eyes when he knew that because there was no one else they would turn to him to be King of Saria.

"Are you ready, my darling?" Juro asked in a low voice as he came into the room.

"Yes . . . yes . . . I am ready," Aldrina said, "and . . . thank you for . . . the wreath."

"You look even more like Aphrodite than you did before," he said, "and there is a bouquet of the same flowers waiting for you in the carriage."

"Thank . . . you," Aldrina said in a whisper.

He took her hand in his and drew her down the corridor and up the companion-way.

There was no one waiting on deck, and she thought that Juro was deliberately keeping them from being stared at.

They went down the gang-plank to where there was a carriage drawn by two white horses.

Juro helped Aldrina into it.

As she sat down on the back seat she saw the bouquet he had told her was made up of the same flowers as her wreath.

She smiled at him and he said:

"We must think of nothing at this moment except our love. We were meant for each other by God, and therefore God will bless our marriage. We will find the real happiness that all men seek but few are fortunate enough to find."

What Juro said made her feel the same rapture as the Gypsy music had aroused in her.

The world seemed to have melted away into nothingness.

There was only Juro — Juro's eyes looking into hers and his heart lifting her up to the sky.

They drove for only a few minutes, but she did not look to see where they were going, or even think about it.

When the horses came to a standstill, she saw they were in front of a small Chapel or Church.

There was a stone cross above the door which was standing open.

Juro helped her out of the carriage and they walked up the few steps and into the strangest Church Aldrina had ever seen.

Above them on the ceiling and over the walls were hanging fishing nets.

At the far end of the little Church there was an altar ablaze with candles and seven silver lamps hanging in front of it.

The Priest was not wearing the elaborate robes that the Priest had worn the night before.

He wore a simple surplice, and Aldrina

saw he was an old man with a white beard.

As Juro and Aldrina reached him, he said in a very deep and sincere voice:

"Welcome, my children, to the house of God, where He will bless you."

He began the Marriage Service and now Aldrina was married as Mary Drina and Juro was Miklos Alexander.

She thought the names suited him, and every word of the Service was said with sincerity.

It made her feel as if the little Church were filled with angels.

The stars that had guided her seemed to be shining their light on both her and Juro.

The ring she had been given last night had been taken away from her with the Crown Jewels.

To her delight, Juro produced a small gold ring which he put on her third finger.

They knelt for the blessing and Aldrina was quite certain that God was really blessing them.

The stars that had guided her all her life had led her to this moment.

Whatever the penalties might be for having married a man who was not Royal, he was, however, part of her life.

After the blessing the Priest turned and knelt at the altar and Juro drew

Aldrina to her feet.

For a moment he just looked down at her, then he said quietly:

"God has given you to me, and I will serve you, protect you, and love you from now unto Eternity."

He kissed her gently, a kiss without passion.

But she knew it was a seal to his vow.

He had offered her his life, and no man could do more.

They walked down the aisle.

Before they reached the door, Juro stopped, and she saw in front of them a very beautiful statue of the Virgin Mary.

Without his speaking, she knew what he wanted her to do.

She placed her bouquet at the foot of the statue and, bending forward, kissed the feet of the virgin.

Juro did the same, and they walked out of the strange little Church with its fishing-nets into the sunshine.

It was then that Aldrina saw that it was at the very end of the quay.

She realised that the Church was used by the fisherfolk.

The feeling of sanctity came from the faith of their wives and children, who prayed for the safety of their men when they went to sea.

They got back in the carriage to return to the yacht, and now there were a number of people moving about.

She could see the fishing-boats leaving the quay into what she knew was the River Leeka.

She realised that the river had a number of small quays on either side of it where the fishing-boats were moored.

Now many of them were leaving the River Leeka and making for the Aegean Sea.

As soon as they came aboard, the engines started up and the yacht moved out of the estuary.

There was no time, however, to ask questions because Juro was taking her down the companionway.

She expected they were going to her cabin, but to her surprise he opened a door at the end of the corridor.

She saw they were in the Master Cabin.

It filled the stern of the yacht and it had been decorated with white flowers.

There were lilies on either side of the bed.

White flowers of every description were scattered over the fitted furniture.

Also there were roses and orchids on the bed itself.

It was so beautiful that Aldrina gave a cry of delight.

Then Juro's arms were around her, and he was kissing her wildly, passionately, possessively.

It was as if his self-control had broken and he had been afraid of losing her.

'I love you!' she wanted to say.

But he was sweeping her into the sky and the stars were round them and within them.

It was impossible for either of them to speak, but only to feel in their hearts and souls.

A long time later Aldrina stirred against Juro, and because she was so happy she said:

"I am sure . . . this is a . . . dream."

"That is what I have been thinking myself," he replied. "My darling, I love you!"

"It was as if you carried me up to Heaven," Aldrina said dreamily. "I did not know it was possible to feel so happy, or that love was so . . . wonderful!"

He pulled her a little closer to him, and his lips were moving over the softness of her skin.

"That is what I wanted you to feel," he said. "Am I the first man to have ever kissed you?"

Aldrina gave a little laugh.

"Of course you are! I knew no men until I came to Saria."

"When was that?" Juro asked.

Then he went on:

"I have so much to learn about you, my beautiful little wife, but the only thing that really matters is that you are mine, and now you can never escape from me."

"I would never want to do that," Aldrina said.

At the same time, she felt a little shiver of fear, just in case something she had not foreseen forced them to part.

Then she told herself she was being needlessly fearful.

She was Juro's wife, and that was a bond that no one could break

As she moved her hand she saw the ring on her finger flash in the sunlight and she asked:

"How can you have found a real wedding-ring for me?"

"It was my Mother's," Juro explained. "I have always kept it in the box in which I keep my cuff-links, so it travels everywhere with me."

"I am very, very . . . proud to wear . . . your Mother's ring," Aldrina said.

"And she would say that you are exactly

the wife she would want for me," Juro answered.

His hands were moving along her body, and he said:

"How can I tell you how much I love you and how perfect you are in every way?"

"Tell me . . . please . . . tell me," Aldrina begged, "otherwise I shall always be afraid that you may be disappointed."

Juro gave a little laugh.

"That would be impossible. How could anyone be disappointed in Aphrodite?"

Aldrina put up her hand to touch his face.

"And you are exactly like the man I have dreamed of and hoped that one day I would find. My dream-man looked like Apollo, and that is how you look."

"Go on thinking that for the rest of our lives," Juro begged.

Then he was kissing her, kissing her so passionately that she felt the stars in her breast turn to flames of fire.

It seemed to her that they were both burning with the magic which made them no longer human but one with the gods.

Somehow Aldrina could never remember later exactly what food they ate, but Juro assured her it was the ambrosia and the nectar of the gods.

Surrounded by flowers, they made love, rested, then made love again.

Aldrina felt as if Juro had carried her up into the peaks of ecstasy.

They were in their own Dream-world, where nothing could disturb or harm them.

It was late in the afternoon when, lying close in Juro's arms, Aldrina realised that the engines had stopped and the anchor was being let down.

"Where are we?" she asked.

"Outside your Villa, my precious," Juro answered.

It was something she had not expected, and she gave a little cry.

"Oh, no! I do not . . . want to . . . go back there . . . I do not . . . want to . . . lose you."

He gave a little laugh.

"You are not going to lose me, my lovely one, but I think those with whom you are staying will be worried, and we must reassure them that you are quite safe before we set off on our honeymoon."

He kissed her forehead before he added with a note of laughter in his voice:

"I think, too, my precious, that we will be away for some time, and you will therefore need more than one gown and a nightgown which belongs to the Prince of Xanthe."

"I . . . suppose . . . you are . . . right," Aldrina said hesitatingly.

She was thinking wildly that she had not yet told Juro who she was.

She was frightened, of course she was frightened, that he might be angry.

"It will spoil our happiness if he is cross or perturbed by what has happened," she said to herself. "Why can I not just stay here as I am?"

But she knew Juro was right.

Of course Sophie, and especially Count Nicolas, would be anxious as to what had happened to her.

She was trying to decide whether she should tell Juro who she was before they went ashore.

But before she could make up her mind he got out of bed.

"Hurry," he said, "because I want to start out on our Voyage of Discovery, which is what our honeymoon will be."

She looked at him questioningly, and he explained:

"I have a great deal to discover about my beautiful wife, and I hope she is interested enough to be curious about me."

Then before Aldrina could answer, he left the cabin.

She put on her white muslin gown which Juro had taken off her when they returned from the Church.

He had thrown it down on a chair, but fortunately it was not creased.

She thought when she tidied her hair and arranged it in the way she always wore it, that at least it looked respectable.

At the same time, love had brought a new beauty to her eyes and her face.

She could see for herself that it was transformed into a loveliness she had never had before.

Juro came back into the room.

To her surprise, he was wearing the traditional clothes of a yachtsman.

He was dressed in white trousers and a blue jacket with gold buttons.

"You look very smart!" she said admiringly.

"And you look very lovely," he replied, "so lovely that I dare not kiss you. For if I do, we will go back to bed, and there will be no question of our going ashore."

Aldrina blushed.

As her eyes met his, she saw the fire in his and knew that what he was saying was the truth.

When they went on deck she found that

they had anchored a little way to the side of the Villa.

The yacht was therefore out of sight of the French windows through which she had left.

The two seamen pulled the boat onto the beach so that she and Juro did not have to get their feet wet, and Juro helped her out.

As they walked up the path that led to the Villa, Aldrina did not speak.

She was turning over and over in her mind what she should say and what she should do, but could not come to any conclusion.

There was nobody on the verandah.

They walked through the open windows into the Sitting-Room.

Sophie and Count Nicolas were there, and, as Aldrina had feared, Prince Inigo.

She went in first and Juro followed her.

For a moment there was just astonishment.

Then, as all three of them got to their feet, Prince Inigo said furiously:

"Where the Devil have you been? How dare you frighten us by disappearing in that extraordinary manner! I was just about to send the soldiers out looking for you."

"I . . . I was . . . quite safe," Aldrina said.

Then, almost as if she were forced to speak without thinking of the words, she added:

"I have . . . been getting . . . married."

For a second there was a stunned silence.

"Married?" the Prince demanded. "What in God's name do you mean by that? How can you be married? Who is this man with you?"

"I will explain," Juro said in a quiet voice.

"Explain?" the Prince interrupted. "I want no explanations from you. If you think you can marry the Queen, you are very much mistaken, and the sooner the Count takes you into custody, the better!"

He shouted the words so rudely and loudly that they seemed to echo round the room.

Then Aldrina heard Juro say:

"The — Queen?"

She turned and held on to him.

"I . . . I was . . . going to tell . . . you," she cried. "I swear . . . I was going . . . to tell you. It was . . . just that I was . . . frightened you . . . would be . . . angry. Oh, please . . . forgive me. I did not . . . want you to . . . find out . . . like . . . this."

Juro stared at her.

Then, before anything more could be said, the door opened and Doctor Ansay came in.

"You have come, Sir," the Count said. "Thank God!"

"I came because you sent for me," Doctor Ansay replied. "What has happened?"

"You may well ask that," the Prince roared before anybody else could speak. "The Queen has been gone all night, and now she arrives back with some common fellow she has picked up from Heaven knows where and says she is married to him! In my opinion, the sooner we execute him the better!"

As he was shouting the words, Doctor Ansay looked first at Aldrina, then at Juro.

He walked towards them, and as Aldrina turned to face him appealingly he said to Juro:

"Perhaps — I am — mistaken, but . . ."

"You are not mistaken, Doctor," Juro said, holding out his hand. "It is some years since we met, but I have always been eternally grateful for your kindness to my Father before he died."

"Your Majesty is very gracious," Doctor Ansay said.

Aldrina thought she could not have heard what he said.

As she gave a little gasp, Doctor Ansay went on:

"I received a message early this morning, Ma'am, from Count Nicolas, who told me that Prince Inigo had discovered where you were, and in defiance of my instructions had followed you."

He turned from Aldrina towards the Prince.

"Your Royal Highness has acted against my patient's best interests," he said sharply, "and as I have already asked for your carriage, it will by now be outside. I think you should return to the City."

The Prince had been silent ever since Doctor Ansay had recognised Juro.

Now he muttered a lewd oath.

Without saying another word, he strode from the room, slamming the door behind him.

It seemed as soon as he had left as if the sunlight grew brighter.

It was then that Aldrina said to Juro in a very small voice:

"Who . . . who are you . . . and why . . . did you not . . . tell . . . me?"

He had put his arm around her as if he had felt he might have to protect her

181

against Prince Inigo.

Now he drew her closer and said:

"My precious, I am the King of Ravalla, but I thought you would be angry when you learnt I had married you morganatically."

Aldrina gave a choking little laugh as she answered:

"And I was . . . afraid you would be . . . angry because I was . . . a Queen, and I had . . . decided to . . . abdicate."

Juro stared at her as she spoke.

She knew by the expression in his eyes that he wanted to kiss her.

It was Sophie who broke the silence which seemed to encompass the whole room.

"Are you really married, Ma'am?" she asked.

"Yes, we are," Aldrina said, "and, Sophie, I am . . . so happy!"

"I am glad, so very glad," Sophie said.

"I cannot imagine anything better," Doctor Ansay said, "than that you two young people should have met each other and, as I can see by your faces, you fell in love."

"Very, very much in love," Juro replied, "and may I congratulate you, Doctor, on the excellent manner by which you disposed of Prince Inigo. I have always thought him a detestable man!"

"He is certainly very tiresome," Doctor Ansay sighed, "and I am thanking God that there is now no question of the Queen abdicating and His Royal Highness taking her place."

"Because we reign over two separate countries, we will not have . . . to be . . . parted . . . will we?" Aldrina asked in a frightened voice.

"If you imagine I am going to lose you, even for a day, or a minute," Juro replied, "you are very much mistaken, and wherever our duties lie, we will always be together."

"As you have said that, Sire," Doctor Ansay said, "I have a suggestion to make Your Royal Highness, and I think it is a solution to your problem."

"Go on," Juro prompted.

"I am sure you will remember, Sire," Doctor Ansay continued, "that many centuries ago Saria and Ravalla were one country."

Juro gave an exclamation.

"Now that you mention it, I do seem to have heard about it."

"The King who ruled over the country," Doctor Ansay went on, "had twin sons, but because they quarrelled and had no wish to rule together, the country was divided between them."

Doctor Ansay smiled before he added:

"Need I say, Sire, that one of the sons was called Saria and the other Ravalla!"

Juro gave a deep sigh.

"Doctor Ansay, you are a genius! And now I remember my Father saying once that you were wasted as a Doctor and you should have been a Politician."

His arm tightened around Aldrina as he said:

"My wife and I have a suggestion to put to you. While we spend a long and exciting honeymoon, will you work out a plan to join our two countries together, and when we come back will you become Prime Minister of Savalla?"

Doctor Ansay looked stunned, and Aldrina said:

"That is a wonderful idea! You are so clever, darling Juro, and of course 'Savalla' is a perfect name for our country — yours and mine."

"And we will try not to have twins," Juro replied, "otherwise it might be divided up again."

Aldrina blushed and hid her face against him.

Count Nicolas, speaking for the first time, said:

"May I congratulate Your Majesties and say, on behalf of the people of both countries, that we are thrilled and delighted by what you have decided."

He paused and then continued:

"They will regret they have been deprived of a wedding, but they will be excited to be able to participate in a Coronation which will cement the friendship between us."

"Of course," Juro agreed. "And that is something that Doctor Ansay as our Prime Minister can arrange while we are away. Now, as I am sure you will understand, I have a great deal to discuss with my wife, as we have had no time up until now."

He was laughing a little as he spoke, and Aldrina knew it was with happiness.

She herself felt as if a great weight had been lifted from her shoulders.

Now the sun and the stars were shining simultaneously over them and there was no more darkness.

"Will you be all right, Sophie?" she asked. "No one is expecting us back at the Palace for nearly three weeks."

"I shall be all right," Sophie said quickly.

To Aldrina's surprise, the colour rose in her cheeks.

She looked towards the Count, who said:

"I will look after her, Ma'am, and perhaps I should tell you that Sophie has done me the great honour of promising to be my wife."

Aldrina gave a little gasp, and the Count explained:

"I loved her before we came here, but I never had the opportunity to tell her so. You will understand, Ma'am, that it was the main reason that I was so thrilled to be asked to command your bodyguard while you were in hiding."

"I am so glad, so very, very glad," Aldrina answered. "I know you will both be very, very happy!"

"What you must do," Juro said, "is to get married immediately and have a quiet honeymoon here while we are having one at sea. I know my wife will want you with her when we go back to face the music. And it will make things very much easier if you are married."

Sophie glanced at the Count, and he said to Sophie:

"It is exactly what I have been asking you to do."

"I was frightened," Sophie answered,

"but now I can say quite confidently, with Her Majesty's approval — yes, yes, yes!"

Everyone laughed, and Doctor Ansay said:

"I think I should be allowed to drink to four sensible and very lucky people."

"I will order some champagne," the Count said.

"It is something we are all delighted to do," Juro added. "Before we leave, however, my wife has once again forgotten that she will need some clothes on the voyage."

Aldrina laughed and put out her hand to Sophie:

"Come upstairs and help me," she pleaded.

They left the room together and Juro said to the Doctor:

"God has been very kind. I can hardly believe that my 'lucky star' has not failed me. Now there are no problems ahead because I married a woman with whom I fell in love the first moment I saw her."

"It is not only lucky for you, Sire," Doctor Ansay agreed, "but lucky also for our two countries. I hope you will forgive my frankness when I say that Ravalla needs a Queen, and I have been extremely worried as to how Her Majesty could possibly manage to reign over Saria without a man at her side."

"As I have already said," the King answered, "we both need you."

Late that night, when the yacht was anchored in a Cove just inside the North-Eastern Coast of Greece, Aldrina moved a little closer to her husband.

"Have I made you happy, my precious?" he asked.

"So happy that I am still flying in the sky," she whispered, "but I forgot to ask you where we are going."

"Where could we go but to Delphi, to thank the gods for having brought us together?"

Aldrina made a little sound of joy.

"Then I shall see the 'shining cliffs' and be quite, quite sure that you are really Apollo, and not an imposter."

"I am Apollo, and you are Aphrodite," Juro said, "and our Coronation will not be of two humans, but of two gods."

"It all sounds so wonderful!" Aldrina murmured. "But I would be just as happy to live with you in a small house and look after you, and be just an ordinary wife to an ordinary man."

"It would be impossible for either of us to be ordinary," Juro replied. "To me you are perfection, and as gods we can bring a magic to our people as they have never known before."

Then, in a voice of seriousness, he said:

"Doctor Ansay said after you had gone upstairs to pack that as one united country we shall be very much more secure."

Aldrina knew he was thinking of the Russian menace, and she answered:

"I am no longer frightened of the Russians, or of anything, now that I am with you. The stars brought me to you from across the sea, and I know the stars were above us when we were married in that dear little Chapel. Now they will guide us and lead us all through our lives."

As if Juro had no answer in words, his lips held hers captive.

She knew that he was deeply moved by what she had said.

At the same time, he was rapturous with excitement because she was his, and because they would always be together.

As he kissed her she felt once again that he was lifting her up to the stars which were shining over them.

Their reflection was shimmering on the sea. As the glory of them swept through her breast and into her heart, Aldrina knew that they had found the spiritual wonder of Olympus.

It was what they would give their people when they celebrated the Coronation of the gods.

The glory, the magic, and the ecstasy of Love would be theirs for ever.

Their children and their children's children would carry it on into eternity.

About the Author

Barbara Cartland, the world's most famous romantic novelist, was an historian, play-wright, lecturer, political speaker and television personality, who wrote over 558 books and sold over 600 million copies all over the world.

She has also had many historical works published and wrote four autobiographies as well as the biographies of her mother and that of her brother, Ronald Cartland, who was the first Member of Parliament to be killed in the last war. This book has a preface by Sir Winston Churchill and has been republished with an introduction by Sir Arthur Bryant.

Love at the Helm, a novel written with the help and inspiration of the late Earl Mountbatten of Burma, Great Uncle of His Royal Highness The Prince of Wales, is being sold for the Mountbatten Memorial Trust.

Miss Cartland in 1978 sang an Album of Love Songs with the Royal Philharmonic Orchestra.

In private life Barbara Cartland, who

was a Dame of the Order of St. John of Jerusalem, Chairman of the St. John Council in Hertfordshire and Deputy President of the St. John Ambulance Brigade, has fought for better conditions and salaries for Midwives and Nurses.

She championed the cause for the Elderly in 1956, invoking a Government Enquiry into the "Housing Conditions of Old People."

In 1962 she had the Law of England changed so that Local Authorities had to provide camps for their own Gypsies. This has meant that since then thousands and thousands of Gypsy children have been able to go to School, which they had never been able to do in the past, as their caravans were moved every twenty-four hours by the Police.

There are now fourteen camps in Hertfordshire and Barbara Cartland has her own Romany Gypsy Camp called Barbaraville by the Gypsies.

Her designs "Decorating with Love" are sold all over the U.S.A. and the National Home Fashions League made her, in 1981, "Woman of Achievement."

Barbara Cartland's book *Getting Older, Growing Younger* has been published in Great Britain and the U.S.A. and her fifth cookery book, *The Romance of Food*, was used by the House of Commons.

In 1984 she received at Kennedy Airport America's Bishop Wright Air Industry Award for her contribution to the development of aviation. In 1931 she and two R.A.F. Officers thought of, and carried, the first aeroplane-towed glider airmail.

During the war she was Chief Lady Welfare Officer in Bedfordshire looking after 20,000 Service men and women. She thought of having a pool of Wedding Dresses at the War Office so a Service Bride could hire a gown for the day.

She bought 1,000 gowns without coupons for the A.T.S., the W.A.A.F.'s and the W.R.E.N.S. In 1945 Barbara Cartland received the Certificate of Merit from Eastern Command.

In 1964 Barbara Cartland founded the National Association for Health as a front for all the Health Stores and for any product made as alternative medicine.

In January 1988 she received *La Médaille de Vermeil de la Vile de Paris*. This is the highest award to be given in France by the City of Paris. She sold over 25 million books in France.

In March 1988 Barbara Cartland was asked by the Indian Government to open their Health Resort outside Delhi. This is almost the largest Health Resort in the world.

Barbara Cartland was received with great enthusiasm by her fans, who feted her at a reception in the City, and she received the gift of an embossed plate from the Government.

Barbara Cartland was made a Dame of the Order of the British Empire in the 1991 New Year's Honours List by Her Majesty, The Queen, for her contribution to Literature and also for her years of work for the community.